Used to seeing he

lipstick, Dylan found

bed-fresh

him to his

and even

and feminine

er.

"This is beautiful. Thank you for waking me up so I didn't miss it."

Pausing, Alexandra looked down and fiddled with her camera, but he caught the glitter of her eyes watching him from beneath her lashes. Nervous?

That was surprising. Then again, he was rapidly learning everything about her was surprising. Intriguing. Sexy. So why the looks?

With the aurora borealis rolling and shimmering overhead and the water lapping gently against the pier, he found himself thinking things best left alone.

Longing slammed into him.

Dylan pulled off his glove and reached out a hand, slid it along her cheek, into her hair. She was all softness and warmth, her eyes glittering, hair down around her shoulders. Thick and shiny and beautiful. Which is why he had to tug her closer. Why he had to breathe in the scent of her.

Just once.

Dear Reader,

She's the One is the fifth and final book in my
THE TULANES OF TENNESSEE series. What
a family! They've all been strong, interesting
characters. It's been great fun writing about this
family and getting to know them so well. Don't
worry if you haven't read the rest of the siblings'
stories—each book stands alone. Hopefully after
following Alexandra's story and falling in love
with Dylan, you'll be curious about Alexandra's
four older brothers. You can find the other books
in the series online wherever books are sold.

I love to hear from my readers. Please write
to me at P.O. Box 232, Minford, OH 45653,
or e-mail me at kay@kaystockham.com.
Look for more books from me and Harlequin
Superromance in the future. If you want to be
up-to-date about my releases, contests and more,
please subscribe to my e-newsletter, available on
my Web site, www.kaystockham.com, or friend
me on Facebook and MySpace.

God bless,

Kay Stockham

She's the One
Kay Stockham

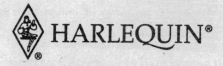

HARLEQUIN®

TORONTO • NEW YORK • LONDON
AMSTERDAM • PARIS • SYDNEY • HAMBURG
STOCKHOLM • ATHENS • TOKYO • MILAN • MADRID
PRAGUE • WARSAW • BUDAPEST • AUCKLAND

Recycling programs
for this product may
not exist in your area.

ISBN-13: 978-0-373-71621-0

SHE'S THE ONE

www.eHarlequin.com

Printed in U.S.A.

ABOUT THE AUTHOR

Kay Stockham has always wanted to be a writer, ever
since she copied the pictures out of a Charlie Brown
book and rewrote the story because she didn't like
the plot. Formerly a secretary/office manager for a
large commercial real estate development company,
she's now a full-time writer and stay-at-home mom
who firmly believes being a mom/wife/homemaker
is the hardest job of all. Happily married for
more than fifteen years and the somewhat frazzled
mother of two, she has sold ten books to Harlequin
Superromance. Her first release, *Montana Secrets*, hit
the Waldenbooks bestseller list and was chosen as a
Holt Medallion finalist for Best First Book. Kay has
garnered praise from reviewers for her emotional,
heart-wrenching stories and looks forward to a long
career writing a genre she loves.

Books by Kay Stockham

HARLEQUIN SUPERROMANCE

1307—MONTANA SECRETS
1347—MAN WITH A PAST
1395—MONTANA SKIES
1424—HIS PERFECT WOMAN
1453—A CHRISTMAS TO REMEMBER
1477—ANOTHER MAN'S BABY*
1502—HIS SON'S TEACHER*
1552—HER BEST FRIEND'S BROTHER*
1587—SIMON SAYS MOMMY*

*The Tulanes of Tennessee

Don't miss any of our special offers. Write to us at the
following address for information on our newest releases.

Harlequin Reader Service
U.S.: 3010 Walden Ave., P.O. Box 1325, Buffalo, NY 14269
Canadian: P.O. Box 609, Fort Erie, Ont. L2A 5X3

This book is dedicated to:

Marlie, for answering *sooooo* many e-mails and questions about Alaska, planes, flightseeing, lodges, etc. Marlie, you rock. This book would not have been possible without you. Thank you so much for your help! Readers, please note any mistake is entirely my own.

Elaine and Jane—ladies, thanks for the help and advice.

And for Glenna. You are missed.
The world just isn't the same without your smile and "Bless your heart."

CHAPTER ONE

IT'S SO SMALL. DOESN'T HE realize size matters? What if he can't get it up, what am I going to do then?

Alexandra Tulane swallowed nervously and forced a confident smile to her lips while she tried to figure out the best way of getting the job done. Climb aboard, close her eyes and pray for the quickest ride ever? Or take things nice and slow?

Slow won't get it up. And isn't the saying, It's not the size but what the guy can do with it?

Her inner voice snickered. *Oh, if that's the case, you'd better hope he's really good.*

Alex pressed her fingers to her lips to hold back a near-hysterical laugh. She'd gone off the deep end. No doubt about it, the stress had finally gotten to her. What else could explain her standing here having a complete conversation with herself?

She tore her attention from the dark-haired pilot striding away from the pathetically small plane outside the terminal window and looked around the airport, trying to stomp down the fear churning inside her. She didn't *do* small planes and the one tied to the pier and *floating* beneath the cloudy late-October sky was just short of matchbox size.

No way would everyone in the waiting area fit on there. What were they thinking? Even she knew planes couldn't fly too heavy or they would—she gulped—*crash*.

In all of her travels she'd been very blessed to avoid puddle jumpers holding fewer than fifty people. That is, until now. From what she could see the Deadwood Mountain Lodge logoed plane only had four, maybe six, seats. It gave new meaning to the word *tiny*.

Her destination was located along Chakachama Lake and touted as being Alaska's guy paradise, "froufrou-less, rustic and lacking fluff." As a writer/reviewer for Traveling Single, she'd reviewed everything from B and B's and inns to five-star hotels and resorts, and had a fabulous time doing it.

But to get to the lodge, was she really going to have to get on *that*?

David tried to warn you but you refused to listen.

Yeah, well, what could her boss *really* know about it? David was a great businessman and had seen the magazine through hard economic times by adding an online subscription e-zine, but he was an armchair traveler. One who rarely left his home state unless it involved Ohio State University football.

Quit complaining. So it's small. Good things come in small packages. Ferraris are small. So are little blue Tiffany boxes. It's even red, your favorite color. How bad could it be?

You'll be riding a scooter in midair—and red just makes it easier for the rescue people to find the debris. That bad enough for you?

Alex shoved the mental argument as far away as possible and focused on the here and now. She could do this. *Had* to do this. After all, she was a professional and professionals didn't balk when met with a challenge. Besides, David would be thoroughly ticked if he'd sent one of his reviewers halfway around the world only to have them protest a plane ride this close to the end.

But you know, considering your vacation plans have been canceled, there's only one way this day could get worse.

Alex winced. She wasn't going to *think* about crashing.

The important thing was to not let her feelings of guilt over missing Thanksgiving with her family get to her.

And how are you going to avoid the lectures come Christmas?

She was an adult. She had every right to *skip* Thanksgiving in Tennessee if she chose to do so. In the meantime, she'd just thank God she would be out of cell range so she wouldn't have to listen to her family's calls of complaint that she wasn't there when the turkey was carved.

Since your plans were canceled you could *go home after the week's up and avoid the sermons.*

No. Uh-uh, no way. She wasn't going to do that. Her canceled plans and pitifully small means of transportation to Deadwood Mountain were *not* some sort of cosmic curse. She'd get there, stay for a week, write a review and spend her two weeks' vacation touring Alaska as intended.

It's an itsy-bitsy, teeny-weeny, red-and-white striped—

A combined panic and frustration-fueled whimper escaped her, echoing off the glass in front of her face.

"Sorry to keep you waiting, folks."

The pilot who'd emerged from the Deadwood Mountain Lodge plane greeted the group with a lift of his gloved hand. He gave them a brief, lopsided smile, and Alex frowned. Why did he strike her as familiar?

The man had a collar-length mop of dark hair raked back from his forehead in a messy, I'm-a-guy-and-it's-just-hair kind of style. A short, neatly trimmed beard covered the lower half of his face and held a distinguished hint of gray on his chin beneath his lower lip.

Never fond of beards, Alex had to admit the facial hair didn't detract from the pilot's looks. He was ruggedly handsome and considering the tiny lines that fanned out from his eyes like he did his share of squinting in the sun, she guessed him to be in his late-thirties.

"Hey, Dylan. How have you been?"

The pilot's expression warmed at the greeting called by one of two older gentlemen waiting by the gate.

"Ansel, good to see you again. Walter." He shook hands with both gentlemen, his tone lowering as he said a few words Alex couldn't make out.

Shifting away from the men, the pilot raised his voice again. "Could I have everyone's attention? Thanks. First off, welcome to Alaska. My name's Dylan Bower, and I'm your pilot as well as your fishing and bear viewing guide during your stay at Deadwood Mountain Lodge. I, ah, just noticed we're missing someone. Well, we'll find him shortly, but until he shows let's get down to business. You three," he said to three men standing off to the side, "are going with Sam here." Dylan indicated another man standing in the background near the gate door. "Sam, will fly you to the spike camp, introduce you to the hunting guide who will be with you the three days you're there, then fly you back to the lodge to finish out the week. So, if you'd like to come introduce yourselves to Sam…"

Dressed in camouflage pants and carrying thick coats, the three men stepped forward. Their luggage included rifles in soft black cases.

From the research she'd done in preparation for her article and review, Alex knew hunting was not permitted in the vicinity of the lodges so as not to attract bear or other animals. A spike camp was typically a series of tents or cabinlike structures set up in a specified hunting area forty-five to sixty minutes away from the lodge. Once the kill was made under the license of a trained guide or assistant guide, the hunters would fly back to their lodge and their prize transported for them for processing. Businesses here had the act down to a science. No meat was wasted, and no animal population overly hunted.

Alex waited patiently for the instructions to continue, and prayed for their pilot to say Sam and the hunters would be taking the red plane outside, that there was a nice, *large* plane to transport the remaining guests to the lodge.

While the hunters and Sam talked, Dylan Bower scanned the terminal again, skimming over her position near one of the airport's metal support beams. In an instant his gaze jerked back to her, and the furrow between his eyebrows deepened at whatever thought shot through his head.

Hmm, not a good sign, that. Instead of the friendly smile of welcome he'd used with the older men, Dylan looked at her as though he could instantly tell she was going to be a nervous flier. No pilot liked that confidence killer.

Tell him size matters, that oughta help.

Squirming beneath the intensity of his gaze because it *was* so direct, her heart picked up speed when Dylan extracted himself from the men and moved toward her with a purposeful stride.

Alex straightened from her slouched position and tried to smile even though her stomach was knotted up like a hangman's noose.

She had to do this. With her family in Tennessee having a baby boom and her mother trying to set Alex up with every single guy she knew—or else badgering Alex to agree to date her lovely but boring, couch potato boss—reviewing the lodge was the perfect way to avoid yet another confrontation about why she wasn't married and pregnant since her brothers had recently discovered love or the joys of fatherhood.

Still, Lord help them all if she died before giving her mother grandchildren!

Her pilot's long legs carried him across the coffee-stained carpet at a rapid pace and when Dylan finally stopped in front of her, Alex had to tip her head back quite a bit to maintain eye contact. He was a tall drink of water. Not to mention attractive. Looking at him wasn't a bad way to spend the week. So maybe if she focused on him instead of the size of the plane, she could get through this?

He gave her a slight smile, one she returned with way too much nervous enthusiasm considering she had a rule about getting involved with anyone associated with the business being reviewed.

"You're not what I expected."

As a greeting, the comment stumped her. *Traveling Single* never announced their visits. In fact, until the review was printed, more often than not the businesses never knew the magazine's personnel had been on-site, which gave the owners or trustee board members or whomever had requested the review of the accommodations true insight from a guest's eyes as well as an unbiased review from one of America's most trusted vacation sources. "I'm not?"

He shook his head and the hint of a smile disappeared. "I thought you'd be older and…"

His gaze slipped lower and in response her body warmed. All from a look. She'd heard about that happening and read about experiencing such a thing in her favorite beach reads but it had never actually happened *to* her. And despite the thrill, a sense of unease followed it because the good girl in her knew mixing business with pleasure wasn't smart.

Alex shifted her weight and tried to regain a friendly yet professional demeanor versus the one inside her shrieking, *Go for it, he's soooo hot!* "Excuse me? I'm afraid I'm not following you."

His gaze narrowed even more at her obvious confusion before he scanned the terminal once again, his eyes searching every nook and cranny before finally focusing on the clipboard in his hand. Several seconds passed before he said, "You're not her." A somewhat heavy sigh escaped him. "Says here she graduated high school in '84 and you're not— Well, sorry to bother you. My mistake."

"Wait." He'd turned to go and she reached out to stop him, laying her hand on his forearm. In the process his coat sleeve scrunched up above his glove, revealing a red patch of skin covered in painful-looking scars.

Alex froze. She'd spent every summer of her teen years volunteering at the hospital in Tennessee where her father practiced medicine, and she recognized burn wounds when she saw them.

Dylan shrugged off her touch and yanked the sleeve down.

Oh, the poor guy. One glance told her he wasn't comfortable with what had just happened and an apology would be met with great unease. In an instant she decided it better to pretend the incident hadn't occurred, that she hadn't seen the scars and therefore couldn't acknowledge them. And why would she? A few scars didn't make or break a man. "Not her, *who?*" she asked. "Who are you looking for?"

He hesitated a long, tension-filled moment before answering. "The housekeeper-nanny, Ms. Johnson."

Alex was struck by the beautiful hazel color of his eyes before she focused on one word—*nanny.* Her brother Ethan had recently hired a nanny. Maybe it was an assumption, but the only reason for Dylan searching the small terminal for one was if he had a child.

The smidge of interest she'd felt at spending the week hanging around the lodge with him dimmed at the news. No doubt Dylan Bower had a cute kid and an adoring wife waiting for him at home, and unlike others in her profession who hooked up whenever, wherever and with whomever regardless of marital status, she wasn't the type to encroach on another woman's man. "Ah, I see. No, I'm not Ms. Johnson."

Something darkened his eyes. "Like I said, sorry about the mix-up."

Just like that he left her standing there. No word of goodbye, not even a request to join the other guests.

Taken aback, she blinked. How strange. Then again,

maybe he'd seen her interest wane at the mention of his nanny? Or maybe she should have acknowledged his scars? Who knew?

The man had his hands full, and was obviously worried about his missing housekeeper as well as the other lodge guests. He didn't need her fussing over a silly blunder when he was undoubtedly feeling the impact of the delay on his schedule.

"Folks? Do me a favor and stay in this area while I try to round up a couple missing people." Dylan snagged something off his clipboard and handed the sheets to the men, instructing them to fill out the papers and sign them before he moved on to hunt for his elusive passengers.

Her inner child huffed at the slight. What about her? He'd had those slips when he'd approached her. Didn't she need to sign one of those papers?

It probably confirms your next of kin. You really wanna sign that?

She shook her head at her sarcastic inner self. She really needed to start focusing more on positive self-talk.

Her gaze landed on Dylan once more. Or rather his nice, tight tush as he stepped off the carpeted waiting area onto the concourse floor, his head high and foot-steps ringing with the sharp sound of authority and— *niiice.* She recognized the maker of those boots.

Years ago she and her four older brothers had gone together to purchase a pair of Lucchese boots for her father for Christmas after he'd read about the boots and admired them. She'd taken a crash course on leather-work and the nuances of their distinctive style. Like those her father now wore for family gatherings or special events, the boots on Dylan's feet were Western, hand-tooled, expensive and totally at odds with the waterproof boots, sneakers and loafers she'd seen worn by men here so far. But why would an Alaskan bush pilot catering to fishing expeditions have boots like that?

Maybe for the same reason a doctor in Tennessee has them? Because he likes them? Wanted them?

Dylan spoke briefly with the airline attendant at the closest desk. The attendant searched her counter then handed him a note along with a smile Dylan seemed to ignore.

After reading the note, Dylan crumpled the paper in his gloved fist before tossing it into the closest waste can. Whatever had been in that note hadn't been good news.

Dylan paused to say something to the hunters and Sam as he walked by. Two seconds later Ansel and Walter joined them and the entire group encircled Dylan, the sight reminding her of a testosterone-filled huddle more appropriate on a football field.

So, apparently women venturing into this male-dominated terrain would have to be the bold type, otherwise they'd be ignored.

Alex waited to see if Dylan would come talk to her the way he had the rest of the guests, and felt her irritation elevate when he didn't. Sam and the hunters went on their way, but Dylan stayed with the two older men. Dylan didn't so much as look in her direction.

'Bout time for the lone girl to go shake things up a bit, don't ya think?

Her mama had always said she was the bold type.

She straightened to her full height, glad she'd worn her Jimmy Choo boots for added lift to combat her shorter stature. Clothes and shoes were a major weakness of hers but the right outfit gave her confidence and today was no exception. She might long to get on a nice, *big* plane back to Tennessee, but she hadn't traveled all the way to Alaska to freak out over her worst nightmare—or sit on the sidelines while the boys' club ignored her existence.

Nope, fact was sometimes a girl had to make some noise—or in the case of her all-male lodge companions, grow a pair.

CHAPTER TWO

DYLAN TRIED TO KEEP A CIVIL appearance for the guests despite the anger coursing through his veins. The men followed him like puppies, excited about their upcoming adventures and not seeming to notice his mind was elsewhere. He let them talk, taking the time to think of an alternative plan.

According to the attendant, Ms. Johnson had paced a hole in the carpet for all of five minutes, approached the desk to scribble out her apology and excuse, and hightailed it out of there. Even at twice the going rate the woman had changed her mind about the job at the last minute. Question was why? Was it because she'd balked at taking on a five-year-old kid, a stubborn old cuss post-heart attack, plus housekeeping and cooking for the lodge—or because she'd done a little research on him and didn't want to work for someone once arrested for suspicion of murder?

He had a feeling he knew the answer.

Dylan searched the terminal for his missing guest and ignored the woman across the waiting area. She was probably here to visit family or friends and was waiting to be picked up. He didn't care. Her reaction to viewing his scars had been the kick in his gut he hadn't needed today, not when he was already stressed to the gills over leaving his son home with Zeke.

His father was back on his feet after his heart attack but even with Dylan picking up the slack with the flights and fishing excursions, Zeke had his hands full keeping up with the meals and housekeeping. Adding a five-year-old to the mix had all the ingredients for another heart attack.

Frustration ate away at Dylan's nerves. What kind of father couldn't provide proper care for his child? Even though money was often an issue, in this case it wasn't. He hadn't protested Zeke hiring a combination house-keeper-nanny. He'd even upped the wage Zeke offered because the woman would be working with Colt.

Dammit.

"Dylan, something wrong? What did the gal at the desk say?"

Shoving his anger aside as best he could, he focused on Ansel's wrinkled face. "Flights were delayed all over the western U.S. due to a storm front but hopefully our guy is on the plane unloading now."

"And that gal over there? Who's she?" Ansel asked with a nod of his head.

Dylan glanced at the woman again and wished like hell the mere sight of her didn't hit him like a brick. Maybe then he wouldn't feel the sting of her reaction so strongly. The look on her face… "I don't know."

And he didn't want to.

Ansel gave Dylan a sympathetic pat on the shoulder. "Well, stop worrying and go find your man. I'm sure Zeke and Colt are doing fine but the sooner you find that guest, the sooner we can go make sure."

"Good luck hunting, guys," he said, accepting the signed waivers and watching as Sam led the three hunters toward the exit on the far side closest to Sam's plane. "Ansel, would you mind keeping an eye out while I walk down to the food counter? I don't want to miss the guy if he shows up here."

"Don't mind at all. But if by chance you're looking for that guy from Pittsburgh, I say we forget him and leave now. It'd be safer for him," Ansel explained. "All he ever did was sing and scare all the fish away. Thought for sure Walt was going to toss him to the bears last time."

Dylan smiled at the old man's attempt to lighten the mood. "It's not him. Help yourself to the coffee thermos and keep an eye out while I take a look around." He excused himself and turned abruptly only to stumble when he nearly collided with the woman he'd mistaken for Ms. Johnson. "Sorry."

"My fault."

He looked down to see if he had stepped on her and noted the pointy tips of her ridiculously high-heeled boots going toe-to-toe with his Luccheses. At least his boots were comfortable. Why did some women feel they had to walk around on stilts? His wife had always been that way, teetering around with her toes pinched and miserable, all for the sake of fashion. "I probably hurt your feet stepping on them like that."

"No, you missed me. Look, I know we need to get going so I was wondering when we were going to get down to business?"

He couldn't hide his surprise. "Pardon?"

Her face took on the slightest hint of color. And since

he couldn't remember the last time he'd seen a woman blush, or known one who still could, Dylan found himself staring like an idiot.

She lifted her chin a notch higher. "Shouldn't I also get the paperwork out of the way?"

It took him a second to switch gears from getting down to business to paperwork. "Those are for guests of Deadwood Mountain Lodge."

"Say, Dylan?" Ansel ambled close and gave the woman a welcoming smile. "I haven't met your pretty friend."

She extended her hand to Ansel. "I'm Alexandra Tulane."

"Ansel Williams." Ansel pumped her hand like a slot machine. "Nice to meet you. This your first trip to Alaska?"

Alexandra Tulane—*Alex Tulane?* He looked down at the clipboard in his hand. The guest he was looking for?

"Yes." Her gaze shifted to Dylan and held. "Like you, I'm a guest of Deadwood Mountain Lodge."

Ah, hell.

Ansel continued to shake her hand like a long lost relative. "Well, isn't that nice? Thought you said you didn't know her. Dylan and Zeke don't get many female visitors at the lodge, do you, Dylan?"

"No." Because the lodge didn't appeal to them. Ninety percent of women traveling into Alaska preferred one of the nicer resorts or inns. They wanted wallpaper and china and sheets that smelled like flowers, not cold floors and men who farted, burped and didn't always shower after a day of fishing.

Once the shock wore off, suspicion set in. He couldn't help it. Why would a woman who looked like

Alexandra Tulane *want* to go to a lodge like Deadwood? It wasn't a matter of cost because there were cheaper places to stay. Flight time, fuel and food had to be factored into the weekly price, which is why Zeke catered to dedicated fishermen and hunters wanting to be close to the action and spike camps but away from the tourists. Not that he could blame them.

Dylan wanted to be away from them all. He wished Zeke would leave well enough alone and stop inviting the world to join them, but even feeling that way he found himself flying his father's guests to the lodge since Zeke was grounded until he passed the flight physical—which probably wasn't ever going to happen again. Zeke had been damned lucky he'd had his heart attack on the ground versus midair.

Ansel winked at Dylan and gave him an encouraging nod, the kind that indicated Dylan ought to be thrilled at the prospect of a beautiful woman joining them.

"That's Walter over there," Ansel continued when Dylan remained quiet. "He's a retired navy man. We've been coming fly-fishing up here every year for a while now. Those guys over there," he said, pointing to the hunters on their way out the door. "Sam's a pilot, but you probably heard Dylan introduce him earlier. And that's Bill, John and Stan." Ansel leaned toward her and added, "Stan tells corny jokes, so watch out for that one or you might find yourself stuck listening to them all the time. They're after bear and joining us later in the week. They lucked out with it being such a warm winter so far, eh, Dylan? That'll help the hunting."

Ansel nudged him hard in the ribs. Dylan snapped

out of his daze and glanced at his clipboard even though he knew what it said. "This says Alex Tulane. You're not an Alex."

Her husky laugh filled the air. Like before, he felt an unwelcome rush of heat. He didn't want her at the lodge. With his father's health and Colt's emotional issues, as well as his responsibilities until Zeke figured things out, Dylan didn't want or need the distraction of a woman. Especially a high maintenance one who would doubtlessly need a lot of attention if her appearance was anything to go by.

"I'm the *guy* you're trying to find?"

His expression must have given her the answer.

"Oh, sorry about that. I didn't know or I would've spoken up earlier when you approached me. Then again you would have had to give me *time* to introduce myself instead of walking away like that, so I guess we're both to blame."

She said it with a curl to her full lips and a Southern drawl that softened her words and made him think of home, hearth and humid summer days when the only things moving were flies and mosquitoes.

He'd grown up in California ranch country about as far away from city life as his father could get, but he and Zeke had made a couple trips to the southern United States to visit his grandparents when they were alive. The memories were fond ones.

Alexandra's words, edged with his mistake though they were, made him remember his grandmother's admonishments about manners, and how in his stress about being delayed and Ms. Johnson bailing on him, he'd been as rude as Alexandra implied.

"What's going on?" Ansel asked, his balding white-haired head swinging back and forth in confusion.

Alexandra tucked a tendril of dark hair behind her shell-shaped ear and flashed the old man a magazine-worthy smile.

"Just a misunderstanding, Ansel." To Dylan she said, "Mr. Bower, I have no idea how the mistake was made, but surely there isn't a problem? Does it matter if I'm a man or woman?"

"Of course not." He knew to dodge the sexual discrimination rabbit hole. Dylan shook his head to clear it and tried to think of potential alternatives, all the while staring down into two of the most uniquely beautiful eyes he'd ever seen.

"Oh, none of that mister stuff here. We don't stand on formalities, do we, Dylan?" Ansel said.

Dylan shrugged, still staring and unable to stop himself. At first Alexandra's eyes appeared to be blue but closer perusal revealed them to be deep, pure lavender, the irises rimmed with a darker shade and set in a square-shaped face with a pointy little chin that shrieked stubbornness. "No, we don't. Dylan's fine. And I think I know how the mistake was made. My father, the lodge owner," he clarified, "took the reservations from our service over a radio and must have misunderstood."

"I see."

No, she didn't. And he couldn't imagine spending the next week with her. "Look, Alexandra, don't take this the wrong way, but I'm not sure you know what you're getting into here."

Dylan tried to think of a tactful way of saying what needed to be said. Alexandra was a striking woman.

She wasn't classically beautiful thanks to a nose that was too narrow, the tip upturned a tad too much and rounded on the end.

But more notable was that, despite her long flight, her makeup and appearance were perfect. Every lash was coated in inky black, her lipstick a bold, eye-catching red. With her jet-black hair and sun-kissed skin, Alexandra Tulane exuded a raw, sensual appearance. Combined with her body hugging clothes that showcased her slim form in all its attractiveness, she'd drawn attention not only from Sam and the hunters, but from travelers and airport employees passing by the gate, as well.

"Oh? Why do you think that?"

Dylan quickly ran through a list of reasons why she shouldn't stay with them and searched for the sentences to get his point across without stirring her anger. The irony wasn't lost on him. As a bestselling author who'd made his living at choosing just the right words, the fountain he'd always had at his fingertips seemed to be in short supply and had been the past couple of years.

Dylan tucked the clipboard under his arm and shoved his fists into his coat pockets out of habit, even though the gloves covered his hands and the reminders of his past. "Have you ever been to a hunting and fishing lodge?" He didn't give her time to respond, quite certain he already knew her answer. "Some are nicer than others but Zeke's lodge is very plain. Bathrooms are shared, the entertainment *is* the fishing and hunting as well as the animal viewing opportunities—and that's about it." He glanced down and noted the smooth shine on her perfect nails. "Zeke hasn't been doing this long so there aren't a lot of extras, and we certainly don't have room service, a spa or a manicurist."

Her lavender eyes took on a sparkle of amusement. "That's perfectly fine," she said in her sweet twang. She lifted her chin another notch, a small smile curling the corners of her lips. "I can entertain myself—and paint my own nails."

It was more than her nails. He'd spent enough time in New York and abroad to know a designer coat and clothes when he saw them. His wife, Lauren, had owned two closets full of the overpriced stuff.

Only a very high maintenance woman used to the finer things and having her every need catered to would wear four-inch spikes into the Alaska bush without thought to the consequences. She'd sink into the ground and not be able to get herself unstuck, and he sure didn't have the time to be pulling her out or caring for her wrenched ankles afterward. "Alexandra, I think you need to consider rescheduling or letting me refund your money. I'd be happy to recommend a luxurious accommodation more befitting your…sense of style."

"You're discriminating against me because of how I look?"

There was that word again.

"You do look a little soft," Ansel offered from the sidelines, his wrinkled features and scrunched up expression similar to that of Elmer Fudd.

He and Alexandra both turned to stare at the man and Ansel wisely excused himself to amble over to where Walter waited.

Alexandra tilted her head to one side, the glint of a diamond earring sparkling amongst her glossy hair and the hat pulled to the top of her ears. The accessory was sexy, with a bill she wore to the side and cocked at a jaunty angle. But one good breeze and all her body heat would escape through the loosely knitted holes.

He could see it now. She'd be cold, sick and stuck in the mud in no time flat. "All I'm saying is that you might want to reconsider," he said before she could dance on the discrimination minefield.

Women like her wouldn't fare well at a lodge like theirs and with Zeke moving slower than normal, Dylan didn't have time to minister to her every complaint—and without a doubt he knew there would be complaints. Alexandra was similar enough to his deceased wife in her manner of dress that he felt safe making comparisons, and Lauren had *hated* simplicity with a passion, believing camping, hiking or the like too backwoods and hokey for her refined tastes.

"Okay," Alexandra said with a patient if somewhat put-out sigh, "I admit I'm not here to hunt but I'd like to try fly-fishing, and I've always wanted to photograph Alaska. I hope to go home with enough shots to round out my portfolio, and if *I'm* willing to *rough it* like the brochure says, what's the problem?"

A photographer? A string of curses paired themselves together in his head as leeriness surged like a tidal wave. His experiences with photographers were a nightmare only Hollywood could create. With another of his books in movie production, a book tour in progress and rumors running rampant, paparazzi had stalked him in and out of the police station, stretching the truth, altering fact and making up stories and lies that added a new level of torment to his living hell.

He'd left California over eighteen months ago, more than ready to leave what used to be his life behind, and carried nothing with him but his luggage and his traumatized son. He wanted anonymity, obscurity.

He wanted to be left the hell alone. Did she know who he was? Was that why she was here and insisted on staying? "What kind of photographer?"

Alexandra blinked at the question. "Nature, wildlife. Mostly scenic stuff. I sell my photos online to businesses and advertising agencies for promotional materials. Have you seen the photos used for Roo Insurance or the Western States Tourism campaign? Those are mine," she said with a proud smile. "And I'm also gathering photos for a gallery showing in Tennessee."

Not tabloid paparazzi. That was definitely good news. "Sounds like you're doing well," he murmured.

Zeke often told him how paranoid he'd become since his arrest, but how could he not be? That experience, like all the others surrounding Lauren's death, had changed him and not for the better. "But I believe you'd enjoy one of the other resorts or inns along the peninsula more. I'd be happy to give you a refund and help you rebook with another company. We can go do it right now."

"Wait a minute," she said before he could take a step, her gaze searching his intently. "Let me get this straight. In this economy, you want to *give* my business away?"

He heard the challenge in her tone, the incredulous curiosity and disbelief. Protesting the way he was, he was raising her suspicions to a degree that couldn't be shrugged off. "It's not because we don't want your business," he quickly corrected. "You're welcome to stay at Deadwood Mountain but most women wouldn't *want* to stay with us. That's the point I'm trying to make. We're very remote. We've been trying to hire a house-keeper for months and can't get any takers."

It was a spin on the reality of the problem but the truth all the same. He blamed the power of the Internet. Unless they were fans of his work most people wouldn't recognize him or associate his given name with anything of importance. But type his name into a search engine and his bestselling author pen name of Dylan MacGregor appeared—and immediately pulled up pages and pages of listings regarding his arrest and the sensationalism caused by a coincidence in one of his novels.

Two years ago his life had played out like a soap opera on news and scandal sheets all over the world depicting the ruins of his burned home, his books and career, and his arrest and release. Regardless of the investigation's final report listing the cause of the fire as accidental, he'd been painted a cold-blooded murderer who had taken a revenge scene from one of his novels and performed it in real life, seeking retribution by setting his wife and her lover on fire and letting the house burn down to cover the evidence. "I'm just trying to warn you that the lodge might not be your type of place."

"I see. Well, I appreciate the warning," she said, a slight bite to her tone, "but I'm sure it will be fine. I might look *soft* but I like camping, and roughing it *inside* a lodge will be perfectly acceptable."

The tilt of her chin told him he wasn't going to be able to change her mind without making her suspicious of why he persisted. And until she gave him a reason to believe she was there under false pretenses, he couldn't turn her away without potentially opening the door he'd worked so hard to close, for his son's sake if not his own.

Dylan's gaze shifted to the floor behind her and he bit back a sigh. If he needed more proof that she didn't belong on Deadwood Mountain, right there it was. Air restrictions required duffel bag type luggage only, but Alexandra Tulane's luggage wasn't the typical black or blue or gray. No, even her luggage was feminine, a bold red and *quilted*. And instead of rifle bags and preferred fishing gear, she carried what he assumed to be large camera bags and a computer case. Just the sight of them made him cringe.

"So…it's settled then?"

Her drawl rolled over his senses like cotton even though her tone was lined with steel. And out of the blue Dylan visualized Alexandra dressed in a bell-shaped ball gown made of purple silk that matched the color of her eyes, her hair mussed and her white gloves smudged with oil from the pistol she hid in her skirts.

Dylan had to blink a few times before the image in his mind faded away.

He couldn't move. How long had it been since he'd had a story scene come to him? Even before Lauren's death the words—the images that ran through his head like a movie—had dried up.

"Oh, for pity's sake, will you relax already?" Alexandra's face was scrunched into a sardonic frown. "I won't sue you if I break a nail, okay? You've warned me. I've read the brochure, and I'm not looking for a spa or five-star restaurants. So long as I have my own room and some privacy, I'll be fine." She held out her hand and waggled her fingers. "The papers?"

Unable to think of more excuses, Dylan reluctantly handed the form over, swearing to himself when he saw her pale. Ah, hell. He could recognize a white-knuckler a mile away and she was definitely one of them. Unless… "It's standard procedure. You know, next of kin, who to contact if the plane goes down. That a problem?"

He certainly hoped it was. If she didn't sign, she didn't step foot on the plane.

Alexandra swallowed audibly. "No. No, of course not. Why would it be? Just…wanted time to read it, that's all."

Stifling a curse, Dylan watched as she called his bluff and scribbled her information on the sheet.

Damn, but he hoped she hadn't had a big lunch.

CHAPTER THREE

WHY WOULD ANYONE NAME A PLANE after a *water-*loving animal?

Alex's nerves kicked into overdrive when she stood shivering in the thirty-four-degree cold—this was considered a warm start to winter?—and watched while Dylan and the two older men loaded the luggage into the plane Dylan referred to as a *Beaver*.

Signing those papers without letting Dylan see how badly her hand shook had taken every ounce of determination she possessed but she only had herself to blame. He'd given her the perfect out and she hadn't taken it, all because of the money required to pay David back—and her pride.

Her brothers' teasing and torment as a child must have really done a number on her ability to know when to toss in the towel. Like that time when she'd vowed to run away and, wanting privacy, Ethan had dared Alex to actually do it because she kept interrupting him when he was making out with his girlfriend. The oldest of the five kids, Ethan was supposed to be babysitting and playing with her, but after the disturbance he'd said some ugly things only an older brother would say. So she'd decided running away would prove to

Ethan she wasn't a chicken—*and* get him into trouble with their parents. She'd walked halfway down the mountain in the dark before her father found her, and to this day she couldn't hear the sound of an owl without shuddering in fear.

Staring at her luggage being placed on board the Beaver? It was like walking down the mountain road all over again.

The muffled sound of Ohio State's fight song began to play and she searched her pockets for her cell, realized she'd put it in her purse last and began to rummage through it, sensing all three men's gazes on her when they paused in the act of loading the plane to watch her frantic search when the music droned on.

Finally she found it. "Hi, David."

"Hi, yourself. I'm glad I caught you. Did you get the call about your vacation tours being canceled?"

She turned her back to the others and walked toward the end of the dock for privacy. "Yes, I got the voice mail when I landed. Not exactly how I wanted to start my trip. I can't believe my whole itinerary is gone. I should've known better than to book the excursions through one company, but it seemed easier. Thank goodness I'd only paid a deposit and not the full amount."

"Check with your pilot and at the lodge. I'm sure they can give you some suggestions. And before I forget, you're going to Cabo for three days after Thanksgiving."

"Oh, nice. Can't wait."

"Is that your teeth chattering?"

"Why do you think I can't wait?" There was a breeze blowing crisply across the dock and it worked its way through the material of her clothes and sent more shivers through her. "I knew it would be cold but even the air up here is different."

"Says the Southern girl who has spent the majority of the past six months near the equator." David's tone held a highly amused note. "What's your first impression? You should be about ready to board the flight to the lodge, right?"

Shifting so that her back was to the wind, she found herself staring at Dylan. "Yeah. And it's...interesting. I was right to take this assignment. The pilot tried to talk me out of going to the lodge. He and one of the older guests agreed to the point that I'm too *soft*, and said it's too rustic for me. I think a female perspective is exactly what this article needs, something to counter the boys' club take on things."

"Well, to take up for my gender, you do have a certain softness about you."

Figures he'd take their side. "Why do people keep saying that?"

David's chuckles filled her ear. "First impressions are what they are and yours screams—"

"If you say high maintenance I'll reach through this phone and smack you."

David laughed again. "I wouldn't dream of it."

But, she noted, he also didn't finish his sentence and because she was wise enough to know the description might be a *little bit* true, she didn't ask him to.

Alex shoved her hair out of her face and wished her sunglasses weren't buried in her purse. Cold breeze or no, the sun kept playing peekaboo with the clouds and like most light-eyed people she was sensitive to the brightness. She began the hunt in her bottomless bag and muttered to herself when the straps slid off her arm. The bag dropped to the ground, spilling some of the contents. "Oh, fudge, I dropped my purse."

David's laughter picked up again. "I rest my case."

Alex glanced up long enough to realize the luggage was loaded and Ansel and Walter were in the process of climbing aboard. She needed to hurry so she wouldn't hold them up. After her conversation with Dylan, she wouldn't put it past him to take off without her. "I've got to go. I'll send the review first chance I get and call or text when I can, but remember I won't always have a signal while I travel here."

Dylan turned around as though looking for her and from across the dock she saw his frown. The man could scowl like nobody's business.

"Wait a second. Alex, I've been doing a lot of thinking about something lately and— Why don't I fly out there and join you? We could travel together and have some fun. See how things go? You know, with us."

The undercurrent in David's voice made her squash a moan of unease. Her family wasn't the only reason she'd come to Alaska. Her feelings would be a lot easier to express on the phone rather than in person. "David, I don't think that's a good idea. We make great friends. I *like* you, but—"

"But I should take that as a not interested and never will be?"

Bingo. "We're too different. I mean, come on, you just bought a house with a *real* picket fence."

"And you travel so much you gave up your apartment," he said with a sigh that carried across the miles between them and revealed his disappointment.

"What can I say, I'm a couch-crasher," she quipped, referring to her penchant for sleeping on friends' couches or her childhood bedroom at her parents' house when she wasn't on the road, and trying to keep things light. "I know of at least three women who'd love to help you paint that fence every year, too." That was no lie. David really was a nice guy, he simply wasn't the guy for her. "You know it would never work. I'd drive you crazy." When he didn't respond, she winced. "So…are we okay?"

"Yeah, *we* are okay. Can't blame a guy for trying, right?"

"Right." If only she could like him as more than a friend. Doing so would certainly make him and her parents happy. "I have to go. Everyone's boarded but me."

"Stay safe."

"Always. See you in three weeks."

She flipped the phone closed and gathered up her things, her thoughts on David. The wind picked up and sent her lipstick and other items rolling across the dock toward the edge. Before she had a chance to scramble after them, Dylan snatched them up.

He'd donned aviator glasses since coming outside and combined with the dark brown coat and boots, his sex appeal was off the charts. The deep secret *zing* of instant attraction she felt for him was what she wished she felt for David.

"Problem at home?"

"Nope, just clearing the air." She grabbed her tampon case before Dylan could reach for it.

Silent, they picked up the remaining items, shoved them into her purse and stood in unison.

"Alexandra, are you sure there's nothing I can say or

do to change your mind? I wasn't going to mention it but I saw your expression when you signed the form in there."

Great, he'd noticed. Alex inhaled and stared at the mountains in the distance. To a lot of people, Alaska was considered the last frontier. She hadn't made it out of Anchorage yet but she could feel the rawness of the air and she couldn't wait to explore, despite her fear of small planes.

But it was more than that. There was also a sense of urgency, because if she didn't board that plane, if she went home to David and her mother and her family and all their fuss over babies and marriages and she spent her vacation *there,* she knew she'd feel inadequate.

Suffocated.

Trapped.

She loved them all so much but she'd found herself resenting them of late. She had a great life, so why were they so worried about her? And if she was having fun and enjoying herself, why settle for boring and monotonous?

When she married—*if* she married—she wanted someone with her same sense of adventure, who'd travel with her to places she had yet to see. But her parents didn't understand and refused to consider her desire as a legitimate requirement. To get what she wanted she had to get on that plane and keep going, continue traveling. Live her life her way.

With that thought in mind, Alex rearranged the multiple straps and bags on her shoulder and forced a smile into her pilot's unhappy face. "I'm ready when you are."

"GET OUT OF MY WAY!" Ninety minutes later Alexandra ignored the hand Dylan extended to help her out of the plane and jumped to the dock instead, running as fast as she could away from the men so she wouldn't embarrass herself any more than she already had. She dropped to her knees at the edge and promptly lost her lunch.

"Better now?" Ansel asked seconds later, the former cardiologist's hand was gentle on her back as he patted.

She nodded, wished she could toss herself *over* the side of the dock and end her mortification, but instead was forced to accept the hanky Ansel waved in front of her face. "Thanks."

"It's Dylan's. He said to give it to you."

Dylan's. *Great.*

Her best friend, Shelby, had told Alex a story not long ago about how Shelby had upchucked in the rose garden of the country club. Alex's brother Luke had found Shelby and also offered a hanky. At the time Alex had found Shelby's resistance to accepting Luke's handkerchief childish and immature but now she totally understood the sentiment *behind* the gesture.

At least it's not white. That would be way too similar to waving the white flag.

"Maybe you'll feel better after you lie down in your room."

She sat back on her heels. "I'm sure I will." Alex dabbed her eyes, tucked the hair that had escaped the confines of her hat behind her ear, and hoped she didn't look as bad as she felt. The whole world weaved—or was it the dock? "I'm fine now. Really. I just didn't— All that water coming up at us so fast and that *landing.*"

Alex heard a heavy footfall behind her and turned in time to see Dylan's unhappy countenance as he leaned over and grasped her elbow in a firm grip.

"That was a damn fine landing."

She opened her mouth to argue the claim but decided she didn't have the energy. If that was a good landing, she'd sure hate to experience a bad one.

With Dylan on one side and Ansel on the other, Alex found herself on her feet and headed toward shore. Sheer will made her shake loose from both men and tug at her coat, flip up her collar and march toward the ugly green truck loaded with luggage. Putting one foot in front of the other should have been easy but more than once she wobbled when the tips of her high-heeled boots slipped between the spaces between the boards.

Alex glared at the plane as she passed it, noting it was now tied wing and tail to anchors. Thank God that was over. For one full week she wouldn't have to get on the darn thing. She'd made it, and while she felt like death warmed over, at least she was alive. Lesson of the day?

Size *did* matter.

"Zeke got a new toy while we were gone," Ansel said from behind her. "Would you look at that. A Super Cub?"

Almost to solid ground, Alex looked in the same direction the men now stared and saw the object in question. Calling it a super *any*thing was a joke, calling it a *plane* was a joke. She had shoe boxes bigger than that. "How many seats does it have?"

"Two."

Her expression must have revealed her thoughts because all three men laughed.

Ansel and Walter gave her the passenger seat in the truck beside Dylan, and two minutes later they were parked in front of the lodge. Everyone piled out to retrieve their bags but before she could grab her camera bag and computer, Dylan shouldered them as well as her duffels.

"Ansel, Walt, you two are in your usual rooms. If you want to leave your stuff, I'll get it after Alexandra is settled."

Walter harrumphed. "We can carry our own luggage, son. Just get her in a room so she can rest."

Dylan charged up the porch steps and opened the door, and she tried to keep up but couldn't. Not yet, anyway. By the time she made it to the top of the stairs, Dylan was watching her from within the entrance.

With a heavy sigh she took to mean he was still irked with her comment about the landing, he headed right and led the way down a hall. Instead of taking stock of the common living room, she followed numbly, hugging herself to combat the cold. The equator was sounding really good right now.

"Here you go. I could put you in one of the rooms upstairs if you like, but this is the warmest. You seem… cold."

Yeah, well, there is a reason polar bears have fur coats.

The bedroom was plain but held a few surprising touches like a cream-colored dresser and a gold framed mirror above it, a beautiful braided rug on the floor at the base of the old-fashioned bed. "Thanks. This is nice." She dropped her purse, the only thing Dylan had left for her to carry, atop the mattress. "Look, Dylan, I'm sorry about, you know, getting sick. And my comment about the landing," she added wryly. "I'm used to larger planes so if you say the landing was a good one, I'll take your word for it."

Dylan set her luggage by the door and lowered her

computer case into the rocking chair positioned in a corner. "No problem."

Yeah, like he meant that?

He indicated the TV atop a small table on the far wall with a swipe of his hand. "The generator runs from 5:30 a.m. to 10:00 p.m. If you need to charge your equipment, do laundry or want to watch a movie, you have to do it within that time frame. No exceptions."

They didn't have electricity during the night? "Doesn't the food spoil?"

"Not in freezing temperatures." He nodded toward her bags.

"Hope you brought warm clothes, otherwise you'll be stuck in the lodge."

Oh, he'd like that, wouldn't he? Given his ultracool attitude toward her, she'd bet he was perfectly comfortable in subzero weather.

"The television has a built-in DVD player. There are some movies and books on the bookcase. Help yourself."

"What about cable or satellite? Internet connection?" She saw the look on his face change to one of *Oh, here we go.* "I know they weren't mentioned in the brochure but it looked a little out-of-date."

"The brochure is current. We like to keep things simple here."

And he obviously had an attitude about it. The man piloted a plane, surely he didn't have a thing about technology? Some people hated voice mail, some people hated e-mail. What was wrong with knowing how the rest of the world lived?

"The bathroom is the first door on the left. Towels are in the pantry. I'll get out of your way and leave you to unpack. Dinner is at six. Breakfast is at six if you want it hot, and lunch is at—"

"*Six*teen-hundred hours?" she muttered under her breath.

His gaze narrowed on her and despite the queasiness, and the way her legs still quivered, or the fact that he obviously didn't consider her lodge material or worthy to be in the seemingly all-male domain, the *zing* was there.

And darn if it didn't increase her heart rate to *thumpety-thump* proportions.

"Twelve noon," he corrected.

"Ah," she drawled, unable to stop herself from shooting back with, "six *plus* six."

"Let me know if you change your mind about staying. I can fly you back to Anchorage tomorrow morning."

And she *soooo* wanted to do just that.

The door shut behind him and Alexandra dropped down onto her bed, flopping across the top like a fish. What had she done to deserve the guy's animosity? A zing? For Mr. It-Was-A-Damn-Fine-Landing?

Who was she kidding? The man cringed at the sight of her and at this point, the feeling was mutual.

What had she gotten herself into?

DYLAN WENT TO HIS BEDROOM long enough to change into work clothes before he made his way to Zeke's bedroom to check on him and Colt. They weren't there. Colt's room was also empty, several books and toys scattered on the bed and floor.

Frowning, Dylan made his way through the lodge and found Zeke standing in front of the butcher block in the center of the kitchen. "You're supposed to be taking it easy and watching a few movies before your guests arrived. Where's Colt?"

Zeke pointed toward his feet. "He wouldn't eat the lunch you left so I thought a peanut butter and jelly sandwich might be in order. You're late."

"There was a mix-up at the airport." A big mix-up. "And one of your guests barely made it off the plane before hurling."

"Well, if they made it off, why are you complaining?"

Dylan shot his father a glare. Ever since his glass half-full change in personality, Zeke was always reminding Dylan that things could be worse. Everyone knew that but sometimes a man had to let off a little steam.

Zeke harrumphed. "Bad mood today, eh? Well, join the club. While you were gone, I got on the horn and found out why my doc's been giving me the runaround on green-lighting me to fly. Anything you want to 'fess up to?"

His father had to realize his limitations. "You had a heart attack. You have no business being in the air without a copilot."

"Then spit it out and say it to my face. Don't go behind my back and have people treating me like a senile old man."

Dylan ran a hand over his face and rubbed. He'd tried that but Zeke continually insisted he would fly solo again. "I talked to the doc once, right afterward. He must have made a notation in your chart. Since you conned Lucille into snooping for you, couldn't she have looked at the date of entry?"

"Leave my darling Lucy out of it."

"She's not your darling, otherwise she'd take the job of housekeeper and move up here."

"She says she's not ready to retire and be surrounded by a bunch of smelly men. And she doesn't want to give up her insurance. Can't blame her for that these days."

No, he couldn't, but if he was going to have to continue transporting Zeke's guests and temporarily be their guide on excursions *and* perform the maintenance duties on the lodge and equipment, Dylan needed help keeping an eye on Colt. The amiable Lucille, the grandmotherly woman his father had been dating for years, would be perfect.

Zeke flipped another piece of bread overtop the jelly and sliced off the crust. "I can tell you're working up a good one," he said. "I know you want no part of the lodge but I'm in a pinch right now since *some*body went and told the doc not to sign off on my clearance. I'll hire Sam to fly 'em in and out from now on. I'll handle things around here, and Ms. Johnson can do the housework and cooking. That leaves you off the hook, so stop your whining."

Dylan moved until he could see Colt. Ignoring his father's grumbling and totally unrealistic view of his capabilities under the circumstances, Dylan squatted down in front of his son. "Hey, buddy. Miss me?" he asked softly. "Look what I have," he said, showing Colt the book he'd ordered for them. "It's the next Toad story. See?"

Colt hesitated for a split second before he continued playing with his horse.

"We'll read it tonight, okay? Sound good?"

No verbal response, not that he expected one. But Colt didn't give him a physical response, either, other than the brief pause.

The pain of Colt completely shutting Dylan out hit

as it always did. Helplessness and anger came next, followed by grief. How long before he heard Colt's voice again? Wasn't two years long enough?

Dylan set the book beside Colt in case he wanted to look at the pictures and stood. "You're going to have to revise your plan," he informed Zeke. "Ms. Johnson didn't show."

"What do you mean, didn't show?" Zeke's frown deepened to crater proportions. "Who was that woman with you and the boys when you pulled up?"

"One of your guests, Alexandra Tulane."

"But…" Zeke's words trailed off and a confused expression flickered over his features. "Well, huh."

That's all he had to say? *Well, huh?*

"Where'd you put her?"

"In the room you made up for Ms. Johnson."

"Good. I worked hard to make it more girly and comfortable than the others. Might as well get some use out of it. Only caught a glimpse of the woman but she's a looker, ain't she?"

Alexandra *was* a looker and trouble because of it. The last thing Dylan needed was to watch over her when he had his hands full keeping track of the things Zeke wasn't able to handle yet. There weren't enough hours in the day. If Sam hadn't agreed to take the hunters to the spike camp, Dylan didn't know what he would have done.

"She's the one who got sick? Poor thing. You never could land smoothly when there's a bit of a breeze blowing."

He pulled his knitted cap out of his coat pocket and yanked it on his head. "I've got work to do—and it was a *perfect* landing."

CHAPTER FOUR

ALEXANDRA TURNED IN EARLY, slept through dinner and the night and didn't awaken until the next morning. She should probably be embarrassed that she'd been out so long but after six months straight on the road and nearly eighteen hours of travel time yesterday, sleep was the only thing she wanted and something about the cold air, overcast sky and soft, comfortable bed let her sleep like a baby.

She took a hot shower, put on her long underwear and clothes and went back to her room to dry her hair to keep from hogging the bathroom. And since she didn't want anyone thinking she was trying to impress them—or that she was high maintenance—she strayed from her usual makeup routine and went minimalistic before she grabbed her camera and ventured into the common area of the lodge. She wanted to get started on the review as soon as possible, that way she could finish writing it before the week was over and be free to thoroughly enjoy her vacation.

First thing she needed to do was meet her host.

Good smells came from the kitchen so she headed that way. Alex spotted a half-full coffeepot on the warmer and practically danced toward the cabinet to search out a mug. One sip and the scent of the rich brew had her toes curling inside her insulated hiking boots.

Her vanity ruled when she traveled, forcing her to always look her best because one never knew who might be sitting beside her on the plane or whom she might meet in the airport. But these boots were well-broken in and perfect for the temperatures and tromping about when even her vanity knew high heels wouldn't do.

Besides, who was Dylan to judge her shoes wearing expensive boots like his? The heels on his boots had looked to only be about two inches shorter than hers.

She sipped the coffee on her way to the refrigerator, remembering Dylan's comment about breakfast only being hot at six. She wasn't picky. She caught a brief flash of something in the living-dining area and stopped short of her destination. Alex walked to the doorway and searched the empty room. Huh?

Obviously you've gone too long without caffeine and food.

Shaking her head at herself, she turned toward the fridge when something scuffed along the floor behind the couch. No mistaking that. She stopped again. Surely an animal hadn't gotten into the lodge? "Is someone there?"

If it's an animal, do you really think it'll respond?

All of a sudden a small dark head fractionally taller than the couch ran down the same hall as her bedroom, startling her and sending her heart rate into orbit. So that's who it was. Dylan's son? Walter and Ansel had both mentioned the boy during the flight from hell. So where was Dylan's wife?

Interested much?

No, her musings were purely research for her review.

Yeah, right.

Relegating the subject of Dylan and his marital status to the realm of *none of her business*, Alex studied the kitchen and noted it was clean with recently washed dishes drying in the sink. The countertop was neat and orderly, and a pot of something was cooking atop the stove—it smelled wonderful but didn't look quite ready to eat. Spying something covered in the oven, she bent over to take a peek.

Oatmeal, biscuits, bacon, some fried apples. Breakfast was served. She'd meant what she said. She wasn't a picky eater and growing up, her overnight stays at her grandparents' house had often included similar selections. Her granddad might have been a doctor, but he'd grown up a Tennessee farm boy who liked home cooking, and everyone in the family appreciated simple foods as well as they did fine dining.

Alex fixed an apple biscuit and took a bite, leaning her hips against the counter. Outside the window she could see Chakachama Lake and its admirers.

Ansel and Walter were dressed in waders and positioned along the lake's edge. Dylan was the only one with a beard and not in the water, and he was pulling tools from a shed and loading them into the back of the green truck.

Alex finished the last of her biscuit sandwich and downed the coffee, pouring herself another cup to carry with her as she explored the lodge. She took some shots of the interior, noting the aged, wide plank floors were worn to a soft golden-brown sheen. The stone hearth was welcoming and obviously old but well preserved, a low fire in the grate behind the screen.

The sitting area was covered in more rugs like the one in her bedroom, and the couches and chairs had scratches and scrapes from frequent use, but were very comfortable. She made mental notes for her review and headed outside to get photos of the exterior. Her readers counted on the images she provided as much as they did her words. Her reviews were typically photo-heavy, with an overview of her stay and short captions beneath the photos as information filler.

Alex paused on the porch and stared, feeling as though she'd been transported to another world. It was...*beautiful.*

Yesterday she'd been too exhausted and too weak to appreciate the landscape. But now... "Wow." It was breathtaking!

Stepping off the porch, the nature lover in her was glad to see the exterior of the lodge was somewhat plain. An overly ornate structure would have been out of place here, but the rustic lodge was perfect, surrounded by the towering evergreens and snowcapped mountains that stretched up to the sky. The lake rippled against the shore and the water was such a deep gray-blue with little dots of— Were those birds?

She looked through her lens and zoomed in, amazed at the sight of ducks landing to float gently on the surface. Alex captured the moment in rapid succession, enthralled at how graceful and beautiful something so simple could be. She'd grown up around mountains and streams and lakes in Tennessee, but this was *amazing.*

Pausing, she pressed her camera to her face as the ducks rocketed into the air. She could already envision the layout. A two-page color spread, with the peaks of the mountain range taking center stage, towering above the lodge. Filled with a new zest for adventure, she set out to explore.

It was a half mile or more before Alex spotted the lodge's green truck parked outside a small cabin. She told herself to keep following the path because the last thing she needed was another run-in with Dylan, but to do her job she needed to see inside the cabins and get a picture if she could do so discreetly.

The cabin door was ajar, and obviously unoccupied by guests. There was no fire in the potbellied stove, no sheets on the bed. The lodge was rustic but this was downright medieval.

The banging she'd heard outside started up again and was interspersed with curses that came from beneath the kitchen sink. Dylan was occupied.

Alex quickly got a picture of the interior before venturing deeper into the space. "Hello?"

The pounding stopped with a surprised jerk of the feet and legs sprawled out across the floor. Dylan angled his upper body to see her, a curved pipe obscuring half of his face.

She lifted her hand in hello. "Hi. I was out for a walk and heard the noise. Need some help?"

He hesitated for a long moment. "I'd really like to say no but would you hand me the wrench over there?"

Ah. Such classic male behavior. He didn't have the right tool but he'd bang away until the wrong one worked. Her brothers did the same thing.

Alex set her camera safely aside and grabbed the wrench to hand to him. More banging ensued followed by a lot of grunts and mutters. Not sure if she'd been dismissed or not, Alex waited, all the while staring at his hands and conscious of the fact that Dylan's gloves were lying on the floor six inches from her feet, allowing her to note he didn't wear a wedding band. Not all guys did, though, so that wasn't necessarily an indicator.

"You change your mind?"

"About what?"

"Flying back to Anchorage and staying somewhere else."

Oh, here she was thinking of his marital status and he wanted her gone? *Nice.* "Not at all. I'm just waiting to see if you needed me to get that loose for you."

Was he *always* so grumpy? Talking to him was beginning to resemble poking a sleeping bear.

The pounding ceased for a fraction of a second. "I think I can get it."

"Well, if you're sure." *Stop poking the bear!*

"What are you doing out here?"

Restraining a laugh at the forced patience she heard in his tone, she leaned against the single cabinet facing the sink. "Walking, exploring. The usual stuff."

He stretched out a hand to retrieve something lying on the floor by his legs but couldn't quite reach it.

Their gazes met and Alex raised her eyebrow.

"Hand me the grips. Please."

Not quite a request but since he'd added the *please,* how could she refuse? "Here you go."

Their fingers brushed in the exchange. Alex barely felt the contact through her gloves, but in the dim light filtering in through the window atop the sink she saw Dylan jerk his hand as though touching her had inflicted torture.

"Sorry," he muttered. "I forgot."

"Forgot what?" Alex stared at him, trying to figure out his reaction but not having any luck. "Why are you sorry?"

ALEXANDRA'S QUESTIONS MADE Dylan pause. In his experience, either people already knew him and the source of his scars, or they didn't recognize him, saw the scars and avoided the subject—and him—entirely because they were uncomfortable with the sight of them.

Her? She asked questions.

"Now you really think I'm rude, don't you? Okay, I confess I saw your scars yesterday but didn't say anything because that's usually what you're supposed to do in situations like that. But just now you flinched. Did I hurt you? Do you have nerve damage?"

Why so many questions? "You didn't hurt me." Dylan took in the look of concern on her face, the open curiosity, but surprisingly he didn't see anything other than genuine interest. It appeared as though she didn't recognize him, always a good thing. But did his scars really not bother her? "They make some people uncomfortable."

"Ah. And for some reason you think I'd be someone they would bother."

It was a statement, not a question, and she seemed offended by the implication. But one glance at her stylish clothes and the care she put into her appearance and image, and yeah, he'd have banked on it.

"Hmm, I'm going to ignore the fact you think I'm that shallow," she said pointedly, "and stick to the subject. What happened? You don't have to tell me, of course, but I come from a family of doctors and spent my summers volunteering at the hospital from the time I was ten until I graduated high school. I know burn scars when I see them. And I know I'm breaking all sorts of social rules and my mother would be *appalled* but— Do they have something to do with flying in one of those tiny wannabe planes?"

So that's where she was headed with this. She was afraid of flying—or rather crashing and burning. And while he'd certainly crashed and burned, it wasn't by plane. "No, they have nothing to do with flying." He told himself to stop talking and maybe she'd go away but he couldn't help but ask, "Why would your mother be appalled?"

His question brought out a smile that put a sparkle in her unusual eyes. "Oh, my mama does *not* believe in veering from social etiquette. Asking someone I don't know such a personal question simply isn't done. If she were here she'd be tapping her foot and calling me into a corner to talk."

His tension eased when he found himself chuckling at the image her words created. "Even if you're right? They are burn scars, from a house fire."

But why had he volunteered that information? Maybe to test her?

Dylan clamped his mouth shut, tensing again when he heard Alexandra release a soft sound of empathy.

"Oh, relax. I'm not going to go all gooey on you because you're obviously a guy who doesn't like that sort of thing. But I am sorry you went through what you did. Burns are extremely painful."

Her bluntness was, too. That was going to take some getting used to. No doubt *mama* had called her to the corner for a lot of talks over the years. "Thanks."

"For the record," she added, her tone firming, "I'm

not that shallow and they *don't* bother me." She tucked a lock of her glossy hair behind her ear and lowered herself to one knee to peer beneath the sink. "Need a flashlight?"

Dylan blinked at the quick change in topic. That was it? He searched her expression, trying to find signs of deception. He saw nothing to indicate she was putting on a show or pretending she didn't already know the story behind his injuries. The fact that she was a photographer put him on edge and made him leery. Maybe there was actually more grit and sincerity beneath the shiny surface of her than he'd first thought? "A light would be nice. There's one in the toolbox."

From his awkward position beneath the sink he heard her digging through the box. Soon a ray of light filled the cabinet. Dylan focused on loosening the fitting on the pipe, putting all his energy and frustration with Zeke and Colt and the whole lodge business and life in general into the act to keep from looking at Alexandra.

"So," she said, drawing out the word, "why are you fixing the sink if you're Deadwood's pilot?"

He yanked on the grips. "My father had a heart attack not long ago and can't. Do it. Himself." Damn, but the thing was tight.

"Oh, I'm sorry to hear that. I looked for him this morning before I left the lodge but didn't see him. I wanted to introduce myself. Is he okay?"

Dylan tried the wrench again but couldn't get it angled properly. "He's insane."

"Excuse me?"

Swearing, Dylan began to scoot himself out from beneath the sink. "He's not really crazy. He's just bound and determined to drive me there," he said, leaning against the cabinet and taking a break to rethink the complications of plumbing repair. When she looked at him with an inquisitive expression that bordered on amusement, he took a deep breath and sighed. "My father only recently purchased these cabins. The owner sold them right before winter which means he got the summer profits but Zeke took on the work of winterizing them. Then he had the heart attack."

"Ah. Now you get to do it and the piloting," she drawled. "The lodge hasn't been a lodge for long?"

"No. Zeke won a *cabin* in a bet about ten years ago when it was a barely inhabitable shed."

She looked impressed. "It's way more than a shed now."

That it was. It was two stories of hard work, sweat and a hell of a lot of cash. And it was their home, not that Zeke seemed to care. "Only the stone structure in front is original. He added on all the rest and fixed it up. Over the years, Zeke's rented the place out to his buddies from time to time but for the past year he's been working it as a fishing and bear viewing lodge. He bought the cabins because he had the crazy idea of expanding even more."

"And you don't want him to do that? I've always had the impression lodges could be profitable."

"It's not all about money." But to someone like her with her designer clothes and perfect nails, it probably was.

Dylan grunted at the thought, amazed that he was even discussing this with her. Then he ordered himself to cut her some slack because she'd been nice to him. "No offense, but I don't want to live in a tourist trap with a revolving door."

"None taken. I can understand that sentiment. A lot of beautiful places have been ruined that way. But your father also has to be able to survive, right? Make a living? Isn't there a way you and your father can compromise?"

Compromise wasn't a word in his father's vocabulary. And even though most guests wouldn't recognize Dylan or put two and two together, it wasn't a risk he was willing to take. He wanted Zeke to leave well enough alone. "It's doubtful."

"I hate to hear that. What if your father succeeds with his plans for expanding his business? What are you going to do then?"

What was he going to do? Sometimes he felt as if Zeke was deliberately trying to shove him and Colt out the door. How could Zeke treat his grandson that way after everything Colt had already been through?

Dylan thought of the advertisement he'd seen posted at the airport by a local. The land was fly-in only and farther north, deeper into Alaska's interior on the edge of the windswept tundra. "Zeke can do as he pleases," he grudgingly admitted. "I'm thinking of buying a place far enough away to not be bothered by Zeke's guests. But until he hires help I'm pitching in because if I don't, he'll have another heart attack trying to do it all himself."

She made another soft sound of empathy. "That's rough. Pitching in when you obviously don't agree with his business plan is no small thing. But I think it's nice. And I understand. He's your father and you love him, but you need your space," she murmured, her head lowered as she fiddled with the string attached to the end of the flashlight. "Boy, can I *ever* relate to that. I feel the same way about my family."

Since he'd rather she talk about herself than ask him questions he said, "Why's that?"

"Oh, because everyone thinks they know what's best for me." She lifted her shoulder in a shrug. "My best friend says it's why I travel every chance I get, because I want to escape them," she said with a laugh.

She wanted to escape, huh? Maybe they did have something in common. He definitely wanted to escape Zeke's plans for Deadwood. "Do you?" he asked, intrigued by whatever it was that put the expression on her face she now wore.

"Travel or escape?" she asked, not so subtly sidestepping the question. "I *love* to travel. There is such a big world out there and I want to see as much of it as possible. Do you travel? Go somewhere on someone *else's* plane?" she asked in a teasing tone.

"No." Not since coming to Alaska. He used to like to travel and tour the places he wrote about but now he liked the security and safety of his home. If only Zeke wouldn't screw it up. "What about escaping?" he asked, shifting the focus back on her.

"Who doesn't want to escape every now and again?" She made a face and wrinkled her nose. "Listen to me go on and on. I've probably bored you to tears." She handed over the flashlight and got to her feet in a graceful movement. "It would be a shame for anything to ruin the beauty of this place but I understand him wanting to share it. And you for wanting to keep it the way it is. I hope you find a compromise because it's gorgeous here." She flashed him a bright smile. "So gorgeous it makes me glad I ignored your warnings and braved the plane."

"Where are you headed now?"

"I want to look around some more before lunch."

Dylan rolled the flashlight in his palms, not looking forward to crawling back under the sink when he was actually enjoying the conversation. "Stick to the paths."

She'd taken a step but turned her head at his warning, her eyebrows high. "Afraid I'll get lost and you'll have to come find me?"

"Yes."

She tossed her dark head with a laugh and spun on her heel, presenting him with a decidedly nice view of her backside.

"Good thing I have a compass and know how to read it."

At her boast, a jolt of sexual attraction shot through him like lightning. Hot, sexy—and she knew how to read a compass.

Alexandra Tulane was an interesting woman.

All the more reason to know he'd be better off with her gone.

CHAPTER FIVE

An HOUR LATER ALEX HAD MADE her way to the lodge and had just lowered her camera to hang at her side when she turned around to find a small boy watching her, his brown eyes unblinking and steady on her. "Hi, there."

She waited for a response, a smile on her face as she studied the handsome little boy. About four or five, he was all eyes and thick, black curly hair sticking out from beneath his cap, sturdy-looking but thin. "You must be Colt. I've been looking for your grandpa. Is he around?"

The boy stared at her, silent and grim-faced.

Alex walked over to sit on a split log that had been made into a bench. His gaze dropped to her camera and she lifted it for his perusal. "I'm taking pictures," she explained, growing uncomfortable when the kid said nothing. "My name's Alex. You know, you're a lucky kid to get to see this every day. What a view!"

She hadn't known what to expect from Deadwood Mountain Lodge since the poorly designed brochure had focused almost entirely on grainy pictures of former guests' hunting and fishing prizes, but the exterior was a combination of rough wood faded to a silvery-gray, and the chunky, mottled stone scattered about this part of the lake.

If Dylan's father wanted to make his lodge a success, why did he have such a low-key brochure instead of one that showcased the beauty and richness of the surroundings? This place deserved much more attention. Especially since three generations were running it—or at least lived here—however reluctantly. That in itself was its own marketing when so many people favored family-based establishments over corporate chains.

Alex worried her inner lower lip with her teeth, aware of the little boy's scrutiny. "What are you playing this morning?"

Ansel and Walter were at the lake, but she saw no signs of Dylan or Colt's grandfather. When she'd walked by the cabin a second time, the green truck was gone. Were Zeke and Dylan in the house? Should Colt be outside by himself?

You played outside alone all the time growing up.

Yeah, but while both Alaska and Tennessee had their share of bears and snakes and animals to watch out for, she'd had her older brothers to keep her out of harm's way. Weren't Dylan and his father worried about predatory animals? Colt falling into the lake? Getting lost? Hurt? Surely he needed to be supervised.

She gave the kid a smile and stood. "I'd like to take some more pictures. You can hang out with me if you like." It was almost lunchtime so she wasn't going far. Why not keep an eye on him? Colt wasn't her responsibility but wasn't that what any caring adult would do? It takes a village and all that? "Maybe you could show me your favorite places to play and what you like to do. Sound like fun?"

She could look around some more, too, maybe get

some behind-the-scenes details for her review. Helping to keep the boy occupied was the perfect way to get what she needed without being too obvious.

Alex pulled out her toboggan cap. Unlike the flirty little number she'd worn yesterday, this hat was thick and wooly and ugly as all get out but warm enough to toast her head in a blizzard. "Oh, I know what else we could do. How about I take your picture for your dad? For a surprise?"

Standing where he was, Colt was framed by a fat pine and the lodge behind him. The image was eye-catching, but toss in the mountain towering above all of them and the photo was awesome, one she could present to her hosts as a small thank-you before she left. Walking around the interior of the lodge she'd noticed photographs were in short supply.

"Come on, smile. *Smile*," she repeated, drawing out the word in a singsong voice and backing up to get the perfect angle. She snapped away, saying silly things in an attempt to get the dreadfully solemn boy to grin. It didn't work. He simply stood there. "Colt? Honey, is something wrong?"

She waited for him to say something, *do* something, but when Colt's eyes widened and he took off running for the lodge, Alex straightened from her crouched position and whirled around, expecting to find a bear or moose charging at her. Instead she saw Dylan closing the distance at a near run, his face a dark mask of fury.

"*What the hell are you doing?* Who said you could take pictures of my son?"

Alex gasped and stared into Dylan's face, her heart

hammering out an unsteady beat because he was so flipping mad. "No one said—"

"Exactly. No one said you could photograph him. Give me the camera."

"What? *No.*" She gripped the straps in her fist and twisted so that he couldn't reach it.

"Give me the camera."

"Go jump in the lake!" Alex glared Dylan down. What on earth? When she'd left Dylan at the cabin earlier he'd been friendly, even teasing. *Nice.* How could a few pictures cause this type of reaction? "This is a four thousand dollar piece of equipment and I'm not handing it over to someone who looks like he'll throw it the moment he touches it."

Fire practically shot from his eyes. "I want those pictures deleted."

"Fine! But *I'll* do it. Keep your hands off." She held the camera up so he could see the screen and cycled through the shots she'd taken of Colt, sending the digital images into the little trash bin one by one. "There. Happy?"

Oh, if looks could kill. Dylan definitely was *not* happy.

"Why were you photographing him?"

Dylan practically spit the words. *What* was going on? Why was he so freaked out?

Watching him, she realized Dylan was more than angry. He looked almost…scared? Panicked? But *why?*

Because maybe he has something to be scared of?

A fist knotted in her stomach. "I took his picture because it made a nice shot. What is your problem?" she asked, unable to curb her straightforwardness.

Dylan's gaze tracked Colt's figure as the little boy crossed the porch and ran into the house before his full attention shifted back to her. "I don't want my son's picture floating around on the Internet."

"I wouldn't put them *on* the Internet." She wasn't clueless. She knew there were weirdos out there and she could certainly see parents not wanting their children's photos online for anyone to view. But why did it seem as though Dylan's upset was so much more than a simple precaution?

Her instincts were going haywire and the last time that had happened, she'd stepped out of a gelato shop in Italy just before a guy had finished his raspberry cone and pulled out a gun to rob the place. Something was off here, but what?

Then it hit her... What better place for a man to hide than in the middle of nowhere? And if that person was a father on the run with his son?

Dylan didn't want Zeke bringing guests to the lodge, wanted to live somewhere else. Didn't want pictures posted on the Internet. Was it because someone would see them? Recognize Colt?

She thought of all the signs she'd seen on bulletin boards and on milk cartons, and her lungs seized. Could Colt be one of the missing children? "I was photographing Colt so I could give the pictures to you and your father as a *thank-you* at the end of my stay. It's a gesture the families at the inns and B and B's I've visited in the past seem to appreciate. Some people *like* having a professional photographer give them something for free."

Her response clearly stumped Dylan. His expression changing from one of anger and total disbelief to wary suspicion to thorough consideration as he mulled over her words, and finally grudging acceptance.

"I…might have overreacted."

Whoa. A man who could apologize? Not that that was an apology, but still. Even though doubts remained, she asked, "Has that sort of thing happened in the past with other guests? Colt's photos posted on the Internet?"

Call her crazy for pressing the matter but her journalistic curiosity was getting the best of her. There had to be a good reason for Dylan to react this way, right?

Dylan's chest rose and fell with his breathing but whether it was from his run up the incline to the lodge or his continued upset over what she'd done, she wasn't sure.

"Yeah, it has. Which is why I don't like strangers taking pictures when I don't know where they'll wind up."

Her anxiety eased. He was concerned. Dylan was a protective, pro*active* father, nothing else. She couldn't hold that against him. "I sell my photos of landscapes and wildlife, not private photos," she assured him. "I thought you and your father, maybe Colt's mother, might appreciate a professional shot of him."

"Colt's mother is dead."

Dylan uttered the words without an ounce of emotion. He made the statement the way people recited facts— it's sunny today, the sky is blue—*Colt's mother is dead.*

Which was why she knew the words held more pain than Dylan was able to express, so much pain he held his body taut as though braced for the onslaught of her response—or the reality of the fact. She wasn't sure which. "I'm sorry. I didn't know."

He looked away, his expression frighteningly grim. "Alexandra, Colt is struggling with some emotional issues because of his mother's death. My father and I

steer the guests clear of Colt because of it. I'd appreciate
it if you keep your distance from Colt, as well."

Keep her distance? Wasn't *that* overreacting? "What
kind of issues? What happened to his mother?"

*Can't you see that he doesn't want to talk about it?
Take your mama's advice already and* shut. Up.

"Dylan, I realize it's none of my business but—"

"Just stay away from him."

Excuse me?

Dylan started to stalk away but Alex stepped in front
of him, reaching out to snag his rock hard arm. "Wait a
minute. *He* followed *me.* What do I do if Colt follows me
again? You were busy and your father was nowhere to be
seen. I was doing you a favor by keeping an eye on him."

Frustration rolled off Dylan in waves. "I'll talk to
Colt. From now on avoid him and keep that thing
pointed away from him."

Yessir, Commandant. Right now she wished she
hadn't made it off his stupid matchbox plane before
hurling. "Fine. Whatever."

Without another word Dylan brushed by her, striding
toward the shed and the bit of green peeking out from
the other side.

Alex watched him go, tempted to lift the camera and
set the lens in motion for spite. She heard the sound of
a squeaky door opening then the truck's exhaust
chugged out a puff of smoke as the engine roared to life.

Dylan had said she couldn't photograph Colt, but
he'd said nothing about not photographing him. When
she went home to Tennessee and told her BFF about her
trip, she wanted Shelby to see who she refered to.

And, yeah, there was the fact she *really* hated being

ordered around. After nearly thirty years of being told what to do by her brothers and parents and pretty much everyone else in her family because she was "the baby," Dylan Bower snapping orders at her pricked *her* temper.

Dylan drove down the path and was almost out of sight when she lifted her camera, the expensive lens doing its thing and focusing in on Dylan's face in a split second.

She smiled in satisfaction.

Gotcha.

"DON'T WORRY ABOUT DYLAN NONE. His bark is worse than his bite."

Alex was about to step over the threshold into the lodge when the man's voice drew her attention. She looked up and saw an older, grayer version of Dylan watching her from the interior. "Zeke Bower?"

"The one and only," he said, offering her a grin as he dried his hands on a towel before slinging it over his shoulder.

Zeke had a face lined with wrinkles and a twinkle to his light green eyes that was missing from Dylan's. "It's nice to finally meet you."

"Likewise. Did you enjoy your walk? Until you ran into my son, that is?"

She smiled wryly and pulled the ugly cap from her head. "Yes. And I'm sorry if I scared your grandson. I took his picture to give to you and Dylan as a surprise but... Anyway, I saw him run inside when he saw how upset his father was."

"Oh, Colt's fine. But he knows he wasn't supposed to be outside without his daddy or me. I'm working on lunch. You hungry?"

"Famished." She followed him into the kitchen, leaving on her coat until she lost the chill.

"Nice piece of equipment you got there." Zeke paused in chopping potatoes and lifted the knife to point toward the camera hanging from her neck. "What are you going to do with that picture you took of Dylan?"

Busted. "You saw that, huh?" She made a face, feeling silly and sheepish now. "I don't know why I took it. I guess because he was acting like such a butt-head and it ticked me off. No offense."

Zeke got a kick out of that and laughed, waving her words away with a flick of the knife. "No, Dylan can be a pain in the ass when he chooses to be. I understand completely."

She settled her elbows on the butcher block and watched Zeke work. "So are you going to demand I delete it like Dylan demanded I trash the photos of Colt?" She snitched a piece of carrot from his pile and munched on it.

Zeke seemed to take an extra long time to think that over. "What are you going to do with it?"

"My uncle's restaurant has a really nice dartboard." When Zeke sent her a skeptical look, she frowned. "Fine, I won't put it on any dartboards. You're ruining all my fun, though."

Zeke chuckled even as he seemed to take her measure but after a few moments passed, he continued chopping. "Dylan likes his privacy. Can't blame a man much for that."

"No, I agree. In my family privacy is definitely hard to come by. There are no secrets and everybody winds up in everybody else's business. It's a nightmare sometimes."

She thought of her recent fight with Shelby, how she'd stormed out, and applied what she'd just said to that situation. Truth be told, she was the one butting in where she didn't belong. Wasn't commenting on Shelby and Luke's marriage an invasion of *their* privacy? But unless something brought Shelby out of her post-miscarriage daze, there wouldn't be a marriage. Then what? Shelby and Luke were meant to be together.

"Looking awfully guilty there."

"And you read people too well," she said with a sad laugh. "I *am* guilty."

"Of?"

"I had a fight with my best friend before I left. She's married to my brother, which gets sticky because I promised I wouldn't let it affect our friendship."

"Hard promise to keep."

That it was. But somehow she'd manage it. "Anyway, I was just thinking of a time when I would've rushed home and showed her the picture and gone on and on, you know, about Dylan's reaction."

"Can't do that now?"

"We haven't spoken since the argument." She grimaced. "I slammed out of her house and I haven't seen her since."

Hopefully by now Shelby and Luke had worked things out. They loved each other but they were both too stubborn for their own good.

"I'm sure you'll make up when you get home. Sometimes you have to let time pass and emotions fade until they're not so raw anymore. Same with Dylan. He worries about Colt being up here alone and we can't blame him, can we?"

"No, not at all."

"Hand me that bowl?"

She did as ordered, thinking Dylan's father had a way about him that declared he was one of those guys who was everyone's friend. She'd have to add a note in her review about hanging out and cooking with Zeke. Bartenders always got credit for being good listeners but she'd discovered hanging out in kitchens was even better. Some cooks seemed to have a way of finding all the right things to say—Zeke included. "May I take your picture? You look awfully cute in that apron. I'll even delete the photo of Dylan."

"Sure, go ahead. But make sure you get my good side," he said, holding his head cocked slightly to the left. "It hides my double chin."

Alex took Zeke's photo, chuckling at his many comments and antics and thinking how well he and her grandmother would get along. They had the same quirky sense of humor and way of putting people at ease.

Wasn't it funny the way you could travel halfway around the world and still find reminders of home?

CHAPTER SIX

DYLAN ENTERED THE LODGE via the narrow utility room door off the kitchen and washed up, keeping his ears tuned to the conversation drifting to him from the dining room table. Zeke was telling that story again, the one where he'd stepped in as a double on a Hollywood movie set for a horseback riding scene and wound up kissing the starlet.

"So you trained horses for movies?" Alexandra asked, sounding every bit as impressed as Zeke liked people to be.

"Not just me, Dylan, too. He helped me until he went to college. I eventually retired and sold out. It's not easy hauling a horse trailer to sets or studios."

"Don't let him fool you," Ansel said. "Truth is he left because he got old and those starlets stopped kissing him."

Laughter filled the air, Walter's deep, booming chuckle louder than the rest.

"Oh, I'll bet there were plenty of starlets out there willing to kiss Zeke. Finding a man who can ride a horse and look good in his boots and hat isn't easy," Alexandra countered.

Dylan heard the playful, flirtatious nature of her tone and frowned at the irritation that appeared because of it.

He'd spent the day second-guessing himself and feeling like a jerk for yelling at her the way he had. He'd worried she'd sequestered herself in her room, wounded and upset.

Yet here she was, just fine. Better than fine, she was enjoying herself.

He swore softly and scrubbed his scarred hands harder, the sound of her laughter teasing his ears.

"Dylan, you're late!" Zeke called. "Come in and sit down with our guests."

Having dragged his feet as long as he could, Dylan dried his hands and walked through the kitchen to the dining table. The unease rolling in his stomach since this afternoon gurgled even more when he saw Alexandra. She wore a dark sweater, her lips an attention-getting red against her soft-looking skin and jet-black hair.

"Sit across from Alex. No need to stay down there on the end."

Leave it to Zeke to put him on the spot. Dylan had planned to keep his distance from her, not spend the meal staring directly at her. But he did as ordered to not make more of a scene than he already had.

"So," Alexandra drawled, fiddling with her spoon, "do you think I have a shot at seeing one?"

Dylan settled at the table and forced himself to be sociable. "One what?"

"A wolf. She'd like to photograph them," Zeke informed him, his gaze narrowed on Dylan's.

"I bet they'd take one look at her and come out of hiding to pose," Ansel teased.

Alexandra gave the man a smile, tilting her head to one side in a way that reminded Dylan of a Southern belle.

Once again an image popped into his head out of

nowhere. Like the scene of a movie, he saw a packed-dirt floor, lazy trails of tobacco smoke curling into the light cast by the lanterns hanging from rafters, and townsfolk gathered in their Sunday best. Dylan could almost hear the rustle of skirts and stiff leather boots. And see a dark-haired woman in lavender silk who stood out amongst the checked and flowered cotton and gingham.

While the women whispered snidely, men raised glasses in appreciation as she passed, hoping to be the one to lead her outside and proposition the woman brave enough—or stupid enough—to be traveling West alone.

The scene faded, the details hovering in the corners of his mind. After two years of nothing, suddenly the images return? In the past the scenes would have indicated the beginnings of a novel, one of many pieces that would slowly form into words and pages and chapters.

"Posing wolves," Alexandra murmured. "Now that would be a picture. But I'd have to have you along to charm them, Ansel. I saw you carrying in your catch. You certainly had the fish coming out of hiding today."

Dylan wiped his hand over his mouth and got busy filling his bowl with stew.

That part of his life was long over. The words had dried up years ago and he was fine with that. Even if more scenes materialized in the future, they were only a reminder of what he couldn't have, not without risking everything he'd tried so hard to protect.

He'd chosen to set his popular character-driven suspense novels in the Old West because of the complications writing in that era brought. But he couldn't write as Dylan MacGregor and reopen the past to more scrutiny and speculation.

His agent would say he could publish under a different name or holding company, but the reality of today's information age was that there were *always* ways of revealing the identities behind pseudonyms and anonymous copyright. Secrets never stayed buried, and there were certainly no secrets in the publishing world.

Dylan searched the room for Colt and found his son coloring a picture on the floor in front of the couch. As though sensing his father's stare, Colt looked up at Dylan but quickly glanced away.

Damn. He shouldn't have lost his temper like that. He'd have to talk to Colt, but how could he get Colt to understand the importance of keeping his distance from the guests without making him afraid of his own shadow?

Finishing off his stew in a minimum of bites, Dylan helped himself to some of the dried pineapple pieces Zeke kept on hand for a sweet treat after lunch. Fresh fruit was expensive to have shipped and the canned fruit was usually served after dinner.

Dylan watched Alexandra banter with the men seated around the table, looking for any clue to indicate subterfuge.

Maybe the scene between Alexandra and Colt *had* been innocent. But if it wasn't innocent, if she had ulterior motives for being here, it would take time to ferret them out.

"Dylan knows all the right spots for you to get some great pictures. Right, son?"

Drawn into the conversation in a way he couldn't ignore, Dylan shrugged. "Alaska is full of pretty pictures. Catching sight of a wolf isn't easy, though. They're elusive on a good day. Some of the bears haven't gone into hibernation." He poured himself a glass of water from the pitcher on the table. "A few still come to feed on the far side of the lake."

"These are the Neacola Mountains," Zeke added. "We're at the base of the range and the streams flow down from the ice caps and empty into this lake. Makes for good fishing, bear viewing. Moose seem to prefer the opposite bank, so you might get a shot of one of them. It's not a matter of seeing wildlife here, it's just a matter of when."

"That sounds awesome," Alexandra said. "I'd like to try my hand at fly-fishing while I'm here, too. The brochure said you have equipment to loan if needed?"

"That we do," Zeke said. "I'm not supposed to be out in the weather much yet but Dylan will be happy to show you what to do. Won't you, son?"

Dylan shoved a piece of the fruit into his mouth and chewed, unable to say no since keeping an eye on her might be a good idea.

THAT AFTERNOON ALEX BRACED her feet farther apart on the bottom of the lake and cast again. And again. She might be able to see the enjoyment in this in the heat of summer but now?

Didn't think about freezing to death while you fished, did you?

The insulated waders offered some protection, but combined with the cold air she was at the icicle stage despite her thick layers of clothing. But she couldn't quit, not until she caught *some*thing because Ansel,

Walter and Dylan were all watching her, waiting for her to give in or complain.

Not gonna do it, boys.

Ten more minutes passed before she heard someone coming up behind her. Alex turned to find Dylan approaching, resignation on his face.

"I have to hand it to you," he said quietly once he was in range. "You lasted a lot longer than I ever thought you would."

Was that a note of admiration she heard in his voice? She didn't respond, not sure she could without revealing the fact that her teeth chattered.

"Look, I'm sorry I went off on you earlier about Colt."

Ah, a *real* apology? Willing to compromise for the sake of peace, she said, "I should've asked for permission first."

Seconds passed and they stood there, surrounded by water and the not-so silent silence of nature. There was a rush from the stream pouring into the lake from their left, an eagle screeching overhead and a moose calling out in the woods around them.

Alex glanced at Dylan from beneath her lashes, aware of it all but totally caught up in Dylan's presence.

Okay, someone needs to lighten up. "Are you *sure* there are fish in this lake?"

A low chuckle emerged from him at her sardonic tone. She was drawn to the sight of his smile, and startled by the flutter of warmth it gave her.

Dylan wore his smile—and his waders—well. That was saying something, too, because *no one* wore waders well. But dressed as he was in a green-and-brown flannel shirt and a thick coat, Dylan looked ready to take on the elements—not to mention quite warm—while she felt like a duck with ice stuck to its tail.

Forgetting to keep her teeth gritted, she inhaled and thought she heard Dylan swear softly but couldn't tell over her clacking teeth. He moved closer, his voice lowering as if he was about to share a secret.

"Cast toward the left and you might get lucky."

Her mind went all kinds of crazy at that. Brooding, moody or not, she stared into his very handsome face and knew exactly how she'd like to get lucky.

Bad girl! Bad, bad, bad!

She didn't mean it. Not really. But she couldn't hold his boorish behavior against him when he'd apologized and she really should have asked for permission, so… they were back to square one, right? Even footing?

"A little more that way. Yeah. I've seen some doozies come from there. Just cast it low, and be patient. You'll get it."

She'd always liked guys who built a woman up rather than those who persisted in tearing her down. Despite his anger and earlier upset, Dylan was a big enough man to say sorry and acknowledge his faults, and it added to her belief that he was a nice guy stressed to the gills about a lot of things. His son, his father, the lodge and expansion and having to work at the success of something he didn't support.

She understood family stress and pressure and the games it played with the mind, the impact it had. "Thanks."

Dylan stood by while she cast again, and again, commenting on her "natural skill." The lure arched low and long over the top of the lake before dropping beneath the surface. She felt a sharp tug. "Oh!"

It did it again.

"Don't just stand there, start reeling. You've got it hooked." Dylan walked deeper into the water. As she reeled her line in, he gave her a smile over his shoulder that positively made her excitement-jittery knees weak. The man might wear flannel and rubber waders and a scruffy beard that was so Don Johnson circa the '80s, but in that second the fish wasn't the only thing dangling by a hook.

"What's she got, Dylan?" Ansel gave her a thumbs-up from his position thirty feet away.

One hand on the line, Dylan dipped into the water. Seconds later he lifted her fish.

Alex couldn't contain her shriek. "It's *huge!* What is that?"

"Looks to be about a twenty-pound arctic char," Dylan said, grinning and shaking his head at her excitement. "And if you're not interested in processing it to ship home, I say it's dinner."

AFTER GIVING ALEXANDRA a promise that he wouldn't drop her camera into the lake, Dylan took a picture of her holding her prize. She should have looked ridiculous in her waders, her hair plastered to her head beneath an ugly cap and her nose red and running from the cold. Instead he found himself admiring her irrepressible spirit. It showed through her eyes and her expression was reminiscent of a kid who'd scored a five-scoop ice-cream cone. "Proud of yourself, aren't you?"

"Absolutely," she said.

"That mean you're ready to get back in there?"

Alexandra looked at the lake where Ansel and Walter remained then turned to stare at the mountains behind them. "Is there a way to climb up to that boulder over there?"

He looked in the direction she pointed and nodded. "Along the back."

"I'm going to go get some shots from there."

"Want some company?"

She seemed as surprised by his question as he was. But he didn't take the words back. If nothing else, he told himself, going with her ensured she didn't zoom in on him.

"Sure. But I left my compass at the lodge so if you get us lost, it's all on you."

Smiling at her sassy response because *no one* could get lost between the lake and that boulder, Dylan told the other men where they were going while Alexandra retrieved her camera and equipment. He shouldered the weighty backpack for her and led the way along the path, keeping lookout for bears and other animals along the way.

He and Alexandra were mostly silent, concentrating on their footing as they made their way up the incline. Along the way Dylan realized he couldn't remember the last time he'd gone for a walk with a woman and not planned on sneaking a kiss in the woods.

Finally they reached the boulder three times the size of the lodge and circled around to the back.

Alexandra stared at the mass in awe. "Can you imagine the force it took to shoot this all the way here?"

So she'd done her research. "Mount Redoubt is the closest volcano and most recently active, but Mount Spur isn't far. Truth is since the 1760s fifty of Alaska's volcanoes have had some activity."

"Don't tell my mother. It'll give her something else to worry about."

Dylan helped her climb to the top of the pitted boulder and watched as Alexandra quickly set to work, aiming the lens, shifting her posture to change the angle. Fifteen minutes passed, twenty. He'd lost track by the time she was finished and lowered herself to sit next to him.

Alexandra cycled through the images on the camera screen and showed him her favorites. She had talent. The photos really captured the feel of their location.

"It's no wonder you want to keep it from becoming crowded with tourists. It's a good thing it's cold and it takes a while to get here, otherwise it would be overrun. It's why you're here, isn't it?" She turned from gazing at the lake to looking at him. "My granddad would have said it was only a taste of what's waiting. I mean, *look* at it. There's something about the air and the smells and the views that make you appreciate every pebble. The mountains…they're almost like a big hug. Am I right?"

His first impression of Alexandra at the airport wasn't his impression of her now. His concerns about her possible subterfuge at photographing Colt were no longer even present.

To keep from focusing too much on that revelation, he watched as she dug into her backpack and pulled out a bag of trail mix, offering him some.

Dylan took off his glove and held out his hand for her to fill. Alexandra cupped her hand under his to catch any overflow as she poured, the cold of her hand seeping into his skin.

"Can we stay here? Just a little while longer? It's so peaceful."

Dylan stretched out his left leg and got comfortable. The quiet was soothing, the company…surprisingly nice.

For the first time in a long time, he set aside his worries and anger and decided to take the moment, the woman, at face value. "We can stay as long as you like."

CHAPTER SEVEN

THAT EVENING ALEX LEFT the older men out by the bonfire rehashing stories of their youth and made her way into the lodge. She was stuffed full of fish, grilled potatoes and apple pie, and since Dylan had packed up his guitar earlier to put Colt to bed, the fire didn't appeal quite as much as it had.

Between her hikes, fly-fishing and the bonfire, plus the meals Zeke had prepared so far, she'd experienced enough of the lodge to begin sketching out a draft of her review.

After spending the afternoon with him on that boulder and knowing how Dylan felt about sharing his slice of paradise, she felt guilty about writing something that would entice *Traveling Single*'s readers to come to the lodge. But that was her job and why she'd been sent there. It had to be done.

In her room she changed into her flannel pajamas, then pulled out her computer for the first time since arriving.

Work. She needed to focus on work, getting the review done before her personal vacation began, and not focus on Dylan or his reaction. Besides, from the impression she had, Dylan would be leaving his father's lodge soon.

While her computer booted, Alex grabbed her toiletries and headed to the bathroom to wash her face. On the way back to her room, she heard Dylan's voice from within Colt's bedroom and paused.

"What do you think? Toad's a pretty cool dude, isn't he?"

No response, or if Colt did respond, she didn't hear it.

"I think so. Come on, bub, lights out. I'll read the rest tomorrow."

Even though she told herself to keep walking, she couldn't. She leaned against the wall and listened to the nighttime ritual, struck by the sweetness of it.

"Time for prayers."

There was movement behind the door, the sound of the bed squeaking, then Dylan began reciting a childhood prayer in his husky voice. Smiling, Alex closed her eyes and silently repeated the words with him, her thoughts shifting to her family in Tennessee.

"Amen. Good night, bub. Remember what I said, okay? You need to stick close to me and Grandpa, and you don't let anyone take pictures. If you're ever not sure of something or you feel scared or upset, you come tell us. I love you, Colt."

Alex straightened, hurt by the fact Dylan was warning his child because of her even as, rationally, she knew all good parents had the same conversation with their children.

Thinking of her niece and nephews and the baby her best friend had recently lost, a pang of homesickness hit that she didn't expect.

She and Shelby had been best friends since childhood. She didn't want to fight. Alex simply wanted

Shelby to see what she was throwing away by so quickly abandoning her marriage to Alex's brother.

Shelby was right when she accused Alex of barely visiting beyond a weekend here or there. For a while now she'd taken every assignment David was willing to dole out so she didn't have to witness everyone pairing up and—

Colt's bedroom door opened abruptly. Dylan walked out, catching her post makeup removal and sad from her thoughts. "Um, hi."

Dylan closed the door and moved closer to where she stood, his gaze zeroing in on her face much to her mortification.

"What's wrong?"

"Nothing." She lifted her hand to her hair, realized she still wore the headband she used when she washed her face, and yanked it out. "I was just... Sorry," she said with a flustered wince.

"For what?"

Was it only this morning that she'd asked the same question of him? "I was eavesdropping. I heard you saying prayers and I stopped to listen." And think. She missed home.

"What would your mother think about you doing that?" Dylan asked.

"Mmm...that's easy. She'd tell me I was rude. But I have a good reason," she argued, careful to keep her tone low.

"And what's that?"

Maybe it was the dimness of the hall or the mood she found herself in but she didn't hesitate to tell Dylan what was on her mind. "I was standing here trying to figure out if I have what it takes." He looked surprised by her response. And very confused. Poor guy, she was probably putting all sorts of thoughts in his head.

Then as though he read her thoughts, he said, "You mean with your family?"

"Yeah." She wasn't sure how to explain or how he knew what she meant. Whenever she went home she found herself balking at having to always report her activities. No one in her family could do anything without having to call someone in the family to report in.

She knew marriage and relationships of all kinds meant certain considerations had to be given to other people, but it was yet another reason she bucked the constraints of settling down.

She waved a hand at the door. "That was very sweet. You're making good memories," she told him. "The kind he'll always remember. When I was little and I spent the night at my grandparents' house, my granddad used to give me piggyback rides to bed. He'd plop me down and tell me a story, then we'd say the same prayer you said." She shrugged, her emotions regarding the memory and her thoughts of family bittersweet. "I miss him, I miss that feeling of…security, I guess you could say. You don't have that once you reach a certain age, though, huh?" she said softly. "Anyway, know you're making good memories with him."

Dylan had reverted to staring at her as though he didn't have a clue how to take her rambling comments. Right now, neither did she. She only wanted him to know he was a good person because something in her saw the struggle he faced with Zeke and identified with it.

"Are you always so blunt?"

"Usually. Scary isn't it?" She curled her sock-encased toes on the cold wood floor and grinned at him. "And now you look a little glazed over so I'm going to go."

"Don't." Dylan stopped her attempt to duck into her bedroom with a hand on her upper arm.

Alex took a breath, barely able to take in enough air when Dylan shifted his hand to her jaw, his knuckles skimming the contour of her face. He wanted to kiss her, she could tell that, but something restrained him. All sorts of thoughts flew through her head as to what.

His gaze lowered to her mouth as he leaned close. His molasses-slow descent gave her time to pull away but she didn't. This was a man she wouldn't mind getting to know, even while she ignored the voice in her head that cried foul and conflict of interest over the review she had yet to write.

What was a kiss in the scheme of things?

Her lashes drifted shut, her heart rate increased, pounding in her ears. She felt the very air between them charge with that *zing*. Finally their lips were on the verge of touching—oh, so close—when Colt's door opened.

She and Dylan jerked apart like two teenagers caught in the act when the porch light was flicked on by a tired parent.

"Hey, buddy. What are you doing up?"

Colt regarded her with what she was beginning to consider his bottomless stare, his brown eyes sleepy but full of questions and curiosity.

"Come on, Colt. I'll tuck you back into bed."

Alex fumbled for her doorknob and gripped it in her damp hand. "Good night, Dylan. Sweet dreams, Colt."

Inside her room she paused to catch her breath and

purge the thoughts of Dylan following through with that almost-kiss and tucking *her* into bed.

No, no, no. She was here for business, hadn't yet written the review and had only days left before she'd fly to Anchorage to begin her two-week vacation. What was she thinking? And why had she talked to him about her family? It was as though she opened her mouth and blurted anything and everything on her mind.

Alex moaned softly. She could flirt to her heart's content, enjoy her time with Dylan because they shared some commonalities—strange as that seemed—but things between them couldn't go further. It was unprofessional—and a really lousy idea for a lot of reasons.

Moving to the bed, Alex sat down with her laptop. Doing some research on fly-fishing was the perfect distraction.

Except, she remembered, the lodge didn't *have* a satellite connection and she had no cell signal.

Crud.

It wasn't *normal* to be this isolated. Every lodge typically had something, a radio at least. What about Zeke's guests? Not having easy access to the outside world was definitely a strike against the business and one that would have to be noted in her review.

Alex grabbed her camera from beside the bed, removed the SD card and inserted it into the computer to download the photos she'd taken before the generator shut down. The images flashed onto the screen one by one. The interior and exterior of the lodge, the lake, the trees and mountains.

Dylan.

There was no denying her interest and attraction to him. And the near kiss?

Shaking her head at herself, Alex clicked on the button to go back to the photo she'd snapped of Dylan pulling away in the truck after their argument. She increased the size, zoomed in and stared at Dylan's profile.

Handsome and rugged, his face had character. Lines and crevices depicting deep, undeniable sorrow were clearly etched with…bitterness? Resignation? Definite sadness.

Because of Colt's mother?

The only time Dylan had spoken of her he hadn't called her his wife, only *Colt's mother.* So had they been married? Were they separated or divorced at the time of her death? Together?

Alex fixated on the slight hint of a cleft in his chin the beard nearly disguised. She saw not a bad boy, but a masculine orneriness she found infinitely attractive. A man who had lived and experienced things, not just the fire that marred the skin of his hands.

Alex settled more comfortably into the comfort of her bed, never taking her eyes off the photo.

There was something else there. What *was* it?

No matter how long she stared, she couldn't put her finger on what. But there was definitely something…

She'd promised Zeke she'd delete the photo but she hadn't said when. It was a small point but an important one.

Until getting the assignment to visit Deadwood Mountain Lodge, she'd never heard of it, and the photos in the brochure hadn't included any of Dylan.

So what was it about Dylan that made her feel as if she'd seen him before?

SEVERAL HOURS LATER DYLAN rolled over in bed and watched the rolling waves of the auroras outside his window reflect off the ceiling. He was exhausted from the long day but he couldn't sleep.

Alexandra's hallway confession had surprised him and given him a glimpse of vulnerability he hadn't expected to see. She was obviously close to her family but feeling the pressure. It was a connection they shared.

As to why he'd nearly kissed her...that wasn't as easy to answer. He thought of her smile and her spirited comebacks, the fact that she'd seemingly accepted his scars and truly didn't appear bothered by them. Alexandra hadn't flinched when he'd touched her face, unlike Belinda—Colt's former nanny and, at one time, Dylan's friend—who'd averted her eyes and avoided the most innocent of contacts.

But Alexandra's feelings could change. How would she react if she knew the story behind the marks? Would she be so accepting then?

Hollywood-style fame rarely changed. Out of sight, out of mind. But after having every book he'd written turned into a movie on the silver screen and gaining quite a bit of notoriety, was that really the case for him? With the fire and the ensuing drama was he really out of mind? Would enough time ever pass when he wasn't a target for those people who made a living tracking down former rock-bottom celebrities, one-hit wonders and child stars for the sole purpose of populating where-are-they-now reports?

His twentieth book had hit the shelves a month before Lauren's death, his twenty-first and last rushed through production to take advantage of the hype surrounding his arrest and the ongoing uproar created when Belinda sold pictures of him and Colt to the tabloids.

The nanny had also sold photos of Dylan with her, photos that were nothing but shots taken from wrong angles, that implied an affair and resurfaced rumors of Lauren's death being deliberate.

His books had flown off the shelves but one after another, his house of cards had come crashing down, revealing the fact that money couldn't ensure security or safety, and nothing could ever loosen the knot in his stomach that had formed when doctors declared Colt's trauma-induced mutism as no longer temporary but ongoing.

Dylan placed the heels of his palms against his eyes and rubbed. He was tired but sleep was nowhere to be found. He thought of the peace he'd felt sitting on the boulder with Alexandra, and when another wave of light shimmered across the ceiling, Dylan rolled to the edge of the bed. He dressed and seconds later stood outside Alexandra's door calling himself a fool even as he knocked softly. "It's Dylan. Dress warm, and grab your camera. I want to show you something."

From inside the room he heard her respond with a groggy "Coming."

Surprisingly, he didn't have to wait long. She emerged into the hall fully dressed, her jeans haphazardly tucked into her hiking boots, the pajamas she'd worn earlier sticking out from beneath a wooly sweater. Her hair clung to the side of her pillow-creased cheek.

Reaching out, he smoothed the hair away with one finger, wishing his scars weren't as severe and he was better able to feel the texture of her skin rather than only the warmth of it. Thank God he still had full use of his fingers.

"Zip up," he ordered softly. "It's cold out."

"Where are we going?"

"You'll see." As with the walk to the boulder, he took her equipment and shouldered it, pulling on his gloves while she zipped her coat and yanked her hat over her head.

That done, Alexandra reclaimed her camera and side by side they walked down the hall to the front of the lodge.

"Sky's putting on a good show tonight." Dylan opened the door for her, unable to stop the smile that formed at her gasp of surprise. Fool or not, he liked that he could give her this. "I heard you tell Walter that you've never seen the northern lights."

"I haven't. Oh, they're beautiful!" She breathed the words, her low voice filled with awe.

Beautiful. Yes, she was. "Want to take a walk?"

"I'm so there."

CHAPTER EIGHT

THE KNOT IN DYLAN'S STOMACH cinched tighter at her enthusiastic response. He was heading into dangerous territory but something strong, something invisible, drew him.

Dylan led Alexandra across the wooden dock, glad Ansel and Walter and the others were all snoring loud enough to blow off the roof so he and Alexandra could share the experience alone.

At the end of the structure he set her camera gear in one of the two Adirondack-style chairs Zeke had built.

"Wow. Oh, wow. Look at that." Alexandra's face was uplifted, her eyes sparkling.

He couldn't look away.

"It's purple. I knew the lights were green sometimes, but not purple. It's almost pink. Is it always like this?"

The shutter on her camera clicked rapidly before she lowered the device and stared at him as though he'd handed her the moon. He finally remembered her question when she raised both eyebrows, a quizzical smile hovering on her full lips.

"No. This is one of the more colorful shows."

"It's gorgeous. Thank you for waking me up so I didn't miss it."

"No problem. To get the warmest room, you sacrifice a window. Sorry about that."

"My room's fine," she said, raising the camera into position at her eye. "I like being warm and it's very cozy," she said, her words muffled a bit by the device in front of her face.

Alexandra looked down and fiddled with the settings, but he caught the glint of her eyes watching him from beneath her lashes.

Nervous? That was surprising. Then again he was rapidly learning everything about her was surprising and intriguing. Sexy. Why the looks? Unless she was also thinking of what had almost happened outside her room?

The aurora borealis shimmered overhead and the water lapped gently against the floating dock. Dylan stood quietly, staring out at the night and feeling the weight of his loneliness gouge deep.

Longing slammed into him, for Alexandra, for Colt. For more than the life they had right now. But how much could he have when it meant opening Colt and himself up to more pain than they'd already endured? He'd bet cold hard cash that Alexandra didn't know who he was. What if he told her?

A particularly impressive dance enacted overhead and Alexandra laughed at the sight, reaching out to lay her hand, then her head, on his arm as though she wanted a connection to the moment. She lifted her face to stare at him and the battle raging inside him was lost.

Shifting, Dylan cupped her cheek, her silky hair sliding over his glove in a soft embrace. She was everything womanly. Sugar and spice, everything strong. Independent.

Dylan used his hold to tug her closer. He'd craved the feel of her mouth ever since Colt had interrupted them. No. Truth be told, he'd craved it ever since she'd arrived with her prissy luggage, silly hat and polished fingernails.

Alexandra tried to get closer but couldn't quite reach him due to the difference in their height.

He finally claimed the kiss he wanted, quickly becoming pulled in by the taste of her, the sweet tinge of mint and sleep.

The ice-cold tip of her nose met his cheek and Alexandra opened for him, willing and responsive, her tongue meeting and mingling, teasing but shy.

He deepened the kiss with a muffled groan.

Alexandra's hands slid up his chest and encircled his neck, her fingers gripping his hair when the kiss turned into an ongoing caress that changed angles and pressure and intensity but didn't end. The camera poked, uncomfortable and hard between them, a reminder of the past he chose to ignore. For now.

Because it wasn't the only thing uncomfortable and growing hard. After over two years of celibacy, the kiss contained the power of a flare going off, the instant catch of powder, the sparkle and flash of light and newness, the long hard burn.

Their hands were restricted because of their layers of clothing, but the passion was there, instantaneous and full of sizzle with every stroke of the tongue, every nip and nibble and taste. Still, despite the heat they created, he was conscious that she shivered in his arms. "You're cold?"

He whispered the words against her cheek, moving on to taste the tender skin of her neck above the collar of her coat. Another shiver.

"A little. Warm me up?"

It was a challenge and request. One no man could pass up.

Dylan took her hand and lowered himself into the empty chair. Settling deep, he guided her down, glad Zeke had made the chairs oversize after pointing out fishermen weren't always the thin type.

Once Alexandra was on his lap, he snuggled her close and ran his hands up and down her body, briskly for warmth, more slowly to learn the feel of her. His head buried into her neck beneath the sweet scent of her hair. He found a particularly sensitive spot, one that elicited a breathy gasp and the clasp of her gloved fingers in his hair once more.

White-hot heat shot through him at the sound and feel of her response and he claimed her mouth, kissing her with all the desire he felt.

Alexandra was a free fall into unfamiliar territory, beautiful and seductive, an adventure calling to him. Even though he wanted to make the leap, his past kept him tied.

What was he doing? *Risking?*

Ending the kiss, his breath blew white in the freezing air. Dylan leaned his head back against the wooden slats and concentrated to bank his body's desire for her.

After a while, once the urgency he'd felt was replaced with resignation, he prompted her to her feet. "Come on. Let's get you back to the lodge before you freeze."

EARLY THE NEXT MORNING Dylan abandoned the pretense of reading the book in front of him. His dreams of Alexandra dragged his focus to her repeatedly even though he tried to concentrate on the words.

He'd left her at her bedroom door, feeling her

confused gaze boring a hole into his back. What guy kissed a woman like that and then—*nothing?*

He rubbed his eyes, mad at himself. His reaction to her was too strong, especially since there was so much more at stake than sex or his former identity.

"Mornin'." Zeke smiled at him.

Dylan decided he wasn't remotely ready for the day to begin. "Why are you so chipper?"

"Oh, stop your bellyaching before your face freezes like that. Or did other parts of you freeze last night out on the dock?"

Ah, hell. "You were spying on me?"

Zeke filled the kettle and put it on to boil. "Saw the lights and got up to watch. You want oatmeal?"

Tea, oatmeal. His father had been taken over by an alien. The man had eaten eggs and bacon all his life. After his heart attack he'd changed his eating habits— great news in and of itself—but his new take on life included being a harping pain in the ass.

"I already ate."

"Make the toast then, would you?"

Sighing, Dylan pushed himself up from the chair and moved toward the toaster by the stove. He thought he'd escaped his father's censure but at the last second Zeke's gaze narrowed on the book Dylan had flipped cover up on the table.

"Son, how many times do I have to tell you you're not going to find the answer to Colt's problems in a book?"

"It doesn't hurt to read about other cases of trauma-induced muteness like Colt's."

"He'll come out of it when he's ready."

Frustrated and cranky, he swore. "And when will that

be? You might be content to wait on it to happen, but I'm tired of waiting. I want my son back, I want him to be—" He broke off in time, about to say *normal*. But it was true. He wanted Colt to be normal again. He wanted Colt to talk and laugh. But what about their life was normal?

Dylan had to take full responsibility for Colt being unable to do any of those things. Every day Colt remained silent ripped another bullet-size hole in Dylan's heart.

"You need to let things happen as they happen. The docs said it best. He'll start talking again when he's ready and not a moment before." Zeke poured out a measure of oats. "Sort of like you moving on with Alex."

Dylan closed his eyes briefly. He wasn't *moving on* with Alexandra. He wasn't doing anything with Alexandra. "Nothing happened."

"Too bad. She's a nice girl. Get the impression she comes from a nice family, too. Not like Lauren or that Belinda woman who sold you and Colt out to the jackals. Those two played you like a fiddle."

Yeah, like he needed the reminder?

Zeke had never liked Lauren and what he called her hoity-toity ways. As to Belinda… Thinking about her deception set his teeth on edge. Colt's nanny had been a surprisingly good actress at a time when his world had been reeling on its axis. He'd believed her lies, until the day he'd woke up to the fact there had been too many coincidences between pictures appearing in the tabloids and her.

Now that he thought about it, his track record with women wasn't great. Why think Alexandra would be any different once he got below the surface? That reminder might be the key to getting through the rest of the week without being tempted to kiss her again. "I don't want to talk about it."

"Why not? Alex ain't cut from the same cloth as the other two. Lauren and Belinda knew their way around men. I might not know much, but I can tell Alex isn't like that."

That had yet to be determined. Only time would tell.

Which is something they didn't have since she was leaving soon.

He swore again. Things between them needed to end here. There was too much at stake. But what was he going to do for the rest of his life? Surely there was someone out there who could accept him at face value?

The image of Alexandra standing on the dock, her smiling face lifted to the heavens, came to mind even as he tried to block it.

"Son, I want what's best for you and Colt."

"If you wanted that, you'd stop this lodge nonsense. You really want strangers crawling all over the place? I have enough money to cover the bills. You could invite Ansel and Walt and some of your other buddies up and entertain them if you want company, but otherwise we could live in peace."

Zeke shook the spoon he used to stir the oatmeal at Dylan. "I've already told you I'm not taking your money. A man's got to make his own living in this world and work for what he has. Now you said you wanted to earn your keep, and piloting while I'm grounded and pitching in with the fishing tours and such does that. I always intended to rent this place as a lodge and you knew that when you came here."

He had, but he'd convinced himself he could change Zeke's mind. "How can we stay if it means the vultures might find me and Colt again?"

"Maybe it'd be good if they did," Zeke said. "Least then you'd have to confront the past and realize it's over. Everybody's moved on but you."

Dylan had a hard time believing that was true.

"You were news for a while," Zeke continued. "But folks know they can't believe what's said just because it's on TV or in those tabloids. And what keeps anybody from finding you now if they really wanted to? Any P.I. worth his salt could locate you in a day or less."

"I don't want it to start up again."

"I know. That's why I backed off getting a new satellite system because you threw such a fit about it giving folks Internet access. Most guys coming here bring guns and fishing poles, not computers. But what about when they get home? Anybody looked you up and blabbed it to the press yet?" He pointed the spoon at Dylan again. "You don't even know because we can't keep track up here. Maybe they did, maybe they didn't. But it could happen at any time and you need to be prepared for it. Get your head out of your butt and stop blaming yourself because Colt's being stubborn about talking. Surely you can find something better to do. Like go kiss Alex again."

"You just pointed out that she's not like Lauren or Belinda. Doesn't that mean she deserves to know the truth?"

"That's your call. If you think so, then tell her," Zeke ordered. "Or be the man you are and let her get to know you so she can make her own decision. Either way the clock's ticking."

That it was. But what should he do?

Not having an answer, Dylan shoved himself away from the counter and headed to the door to grab his coat off the peg. "I've got work to do."

How did something seemingly so simple get so complicated?

Maybe that was his answer. He didn't need a woman scrambling his brain again. For that reason alone he wanted her gone, *needed* her gone.

"Dylan, not everyone is out to get you. It's hard to trust again after you've been treated the way you have, but a man ain't nothing if he can't see outside himself."

He knew that. He knew it well because that was the beginning of his downfall. For a while he'd been entirely wrapped up in his life and his career, his image, until he'd learned the rich man's lesson of putting material things first.

Now he wondered if he'd ever hear Colt's voice again.

"You called me a fool for dumping my money into this pit, but I needed a fresh start after your mama died. Sometimes we all do. This pit has served us both well, hasn't it?"

Then why risk what they'd built here at Deadwood?

Dylan had to be realistic. With his face having been splashed all over the news, the odds were most women would make snap judgments. They'd never be able to relax around him, get to know him. Instead they would wonder and question the real truth. It would take a miracle to find someone who would believe his side of the story and he couldn't stand the thought of the woman in his life awake beside him, afraid to close her eyes.

But if Alexandra was here only a few more days, how

involved could they get? If she could accept his scars, why bring up his identity?

"Dylan, you suffered a blow but you're still entitled to have a life. Colt's getting older. He needs to start school and there isn't one here."

Yet another reason for him to agree to the satellite system. "I've been thinking about that. You should have a satellite set up, for emergencies if nothing else. Using the radio can be complicated if I'm not here and one of the guests has to try to figure it out. Why don't you go ahead and get it? I'll pay for half and use it to find Colt an online classroom."

Zeke set down the stack of bowls he'd pulled from the cabinet with a bang.

Dylan looked up at the sound. "What? I thought you'd be happy."

"Happy? Why would I be happy about that? Colt needs other kids his own age, to learn to play and to do things away from you and me. He don't need you hovering over him every minute of every day."

Dylan paused in the act of putting on his gloves, ignoring the lurch of fear in his gut. "What are you saying?"

Zeke's green eyes held a brutal honesty Dylan wasn't prepared to see. Surely Zeke wasn't implying what he thought?

"I knew you needed to get your feet back under you but I never intended for you to stay forever. You don't belong here, son."

The comment floored him like a prizefighter's KO punch. His feet *were* under him, at least they had been until Zeke had come right out and verbalized what Dylan had already wondered. Zeke was trying to get rid of him and Colt, thought they'd overstayed their welcome?

He didn't know which was worse, the anger and hurt he felt that Zeke wanted them gone, or the fear of what would happen away from the safety of Deadwood Mountain. Both made it too damn hard to breathe.

Moving to Alaska had been about licking his wounds and protecting his son, getting away. Colt's emotional health was fragile, the pieces only now mending together after being shattered to bits. Hover? He felt he owed it to Colt after missing so much of his son's first two years. He'd hover over Colt forever if it meant making his son feel safe. The kid had lived through hell, survived the very flames of it, and he deserved to have someone care enough to hover.

Sweat broke out on Dylan's forehead and his heart thumped hard and heavy in his chest. He glared at his father, so angry he shook with the force of it. "This is our home now, too. You didn't do this on your own. I've invested time and labor into this place. You want me to uproot Colt again? You're not going to be cleared to fly now and you know it. Who's going to fly in your guests?"

"Like you want to do that for the rest of your life," Zeke countered. "The only reason you agreed this time was because you knew I'd do it myself if you didn't."

He didn't deny Zeke's claim.

"It's time to stop running, son. And kissing that girl last night is a damn good way to start. Don't screw it up by letting her get away when she's the only thing in two years other than Colt that's made you wake up in the morning and give a damn."

Zeke implied a relationship. But any relationship

Dylan could possibly have would be doomed. Zeke didn't know everything. He didn't know the secret Dylan kept, and no relationship could thrive or survive without trust. He couldn't trust anyone with the truth, with knowledge that could destroy both him *and* Colt.

Nothing was worth that risk. No one was worth the risk.

"Don't look at me like that. I never said it would be easy. Just tell Alex what happened and get it out there, see what she says. That girl might surprise you. She's surprised all of us here, hasn't she? I sure haven't heard her complain, have you?"

She hadn't complained. She probably would have stood in that lake all day with her teeth chattering like a novelty store toy until she caught a fish. He admired her tenacity. Her behavior made him think maybe she *could* handle the truth of his past and the problems and headaches that came with it.

But what if he was wrong? Once she knew, there was no taking it back and a part of him didn't want to see her look at him the way so many others had, with fear or horror in her eyes.

Dylan walked out the door without responding, unable to be in the same room with Zeke when so much had been said about a future that seemed so out of his control.

He'd done the right thing last night by calling a halt and leaving Alexandra at her door. True nastiness was people on a manhunt, ready for vigilante justice. True fear? Sitting in a jail cell without bond when his three-year-old needed him most, all because he was considered a flight risk.

Why would he set himself up to fall again?

No, Zeke was wrong. Some things you can face, but you can't fight. Some things you can't outrun.

Dylan went to the dock and readied the boat for the day's excursion, his mind replaying the conversation in his head.

He needed to make a call, check into purchasing that tract of land. Otherwise he and Colt wouldn't have anywhere to go where they'd be safe.

CHAPTER NINE

So HE WAS GOING TO BE THAT way about what happened last night, huh?

Alex tried to be discreet as she glanced over her shoulder to where Dylan sat guiding the boat along the lake toward the farthest end, to where he'd said bears liked to fish. Their gazes locked briefly but Dylan quickly refocused on their destination.

With a determined huff and a silent *bite me,* she faced forward again. Having seen no sign of a bear the other day, she'd looked forward to this excursion and nothing about Dylan's tall, dark and brooding attitude was going to ruin it for her. After all, he was the one behaving badly. It was only a few kisses, after all, so what was he so uptight about?

Okay, so maybe she'd thought they'd had a connection in the hall and maybe she'd thought his kisses were *really* nice, but she hadn't expected the silent treatment and she wasn't sure what to make of it. Was she the only one having fun last night? She didn't think so. So what was the deal?

The deal is he changed his mind. It's over. Move on.

Alex buried her mouth and nose beneath the scarf wrapped around her neck, forcing her body to relax between Ansel and Walter.

Then she saw it. Barely a blur in the distance, a bear fished at the mouth of the lake.

"Look at that," Walter said, leaning toward her in an effort to be heard over the boat's engine but not loud enough to scare the bear away.

She'd read that some bears had become so used to humans they basically ignored the boats and chatter of their observers. Still, Dylan cut the boat's forward motion down to a slow glide, and, other than a glance in their direction, the bear didn't move.

Alex felt Dylan's gaze on her like a physical touch but she didn't look back at him. Busying herself with her camera, she zoomed in, determined to be a professional despite the twinge of hurt and disappointment she felt.

If he wanted to be that way, fine.

Alex watched the bear through her lens. She'd photographed plenty of black bears in Tennessee but the cinnamon-colored one in front of her was full of character and brought out chuckles from her and her seatmates. Time and again the bear dipped his large paw into the water after a fish. And time and again he came up empty. Finally, the bear got impatient, rose onto his hind legs and waited for the perfect moment to pounce. Down he went into the water and this time he dipped his head low to retrieve his catch. All three gave a low cheer for the bear's success.

"You get all that?" Ansel asked.

"Yup. Right down to the first bite," she said with a grin.

They watched the bear until he finished fishing and returned to the woods then Dylan guided the boat around. On their way back to the lodge, Alex snapped a few more photos. They passed a moose drinking at the lake's edge, saw migrating sandhill cranes perched on a tree stump, and her present favorite—an eagle sitting proud high in a treetop. He was so majestic and regal.

At the dock, she stowed her camera for safekeeping while Ansel and Walter climbed out. When she looked up expecting one of the older men to be waiting to lend a hand, she discovered them halfway up the lodge path and hurrying as fast as their legs would carry them.

Only Dylan remained.

He released a disgruntled sigh when he finished tying the boat and realized what had happened. Shifting his attention to her, he held out his hand to take her equipment.

Alex handed it over only because she couldn't toss it onto the dock and risk damaging it. While Dylan set it aside, she began to climb out of the boat using the metal ladder.

"Alexandra—"

"No," she said, careful to watch her step onto the floating dock so she didn't fall, "it's fine. You don't need to say anything, I get it." She grabbed her backpack of equipment and straightened, only to find herself nose to chest with him.

"Because you regret it?"

She could lie and say yes but why bother when she didn't regret it at all? "No. Because I can tell, for whatever reason, *you* do." She sidestepped him to follow the others but Dylan caught her arm in a gentle grip, close enough that she smelled the scent of his soap and the laundry detergent stashed in the utility room.

Alex forced her gaze up—and suddenly she wasn't so sure he regretted it so much as feared it. She blinked at the hint of pain and confusion, the flash of vulnerability she didn't want to see. Because of the hurt he'd suffered when his wife died? Was he still mourning her? Was that why he was acting this way?

Dylan grimaced, his gaze shifting away from hers. "I can feel those old geezers watching us from inside. Will you take a walk with me?"

And get shot down again? It was obvious Dylan had some issues. "I guess I could get my camera out and pretend you're going to show me something."

"I can only imagine the jokes they'd make about what I was showing you," he said with a wry twist to his lips. "How about we take the boat over there," he said, pointing to the white, barkless trees sticking out of the lake's edge like toothpicks. "Would you like some photos of those? They wind around the bend there."

Determined to say no because that's what any smart, kissed-and-snubbed woman would do, she said, "Sure."

Five minutes later they were out of sight of the lodge and Alex still wondered whether she'd made the right decision.

They rocked gently on the surface of the lake, and while she actually did retrieve her camera and take several pictures of the white, weather-smooth trees and their reflection on the cold, murky water, she was ultimately unable to concentrate due to Dylan's presence. Had he brought her out here only to brood again? Seriously?

"I don't regret last night. Not in the way you're thinking."

Okay. That was good to know.

"Alexandra, Colt was three when his mother died in a fire."

Alex blinked at him in surprise. A fire. *The* fire? The one that had burned him?

Her gaze dropped to his gloved hands and, unable to help herself, she reached over and trailed a fingertip over the scars she knew were beneath the protective leather. "Where you got these?"

He nodded, shifting forward on the seat until he rested his elbows on his knees, his focus on the watery grove of trees in front of them. "I wasn't home when it started. We lived at the top of a mountain road on a pretty isolated stretch. We had neighbors but their homes were below us and it was late, after midnight. I'd been away on business and had been for a while. Lauren—my wife—got upset when I stayed away too long. She was upset a lot when I was home, too, though, so I'd begun to take the attitude that it didn't matter where I was because she'd always be upset about something."

He glanced at Alex and she noted his expression was the most open and revealing she'd seen since she'd arrived. This was turning into way more than the aftermath of a few kisses.

Part of her recognized Dylan's words as a hole opening up in the wall between them. One that wouldn't close again. Given his tone and what he'd told her... Was it more than she wanted to know?

"It was no secret amongst our neighbors and friends that we had problems. We didn't get along, had our share of screaming matches and we'd separated a couple times both before and after Colt was born." His head lowered another inch. "We had different views on everything, were incompatible, but we both had our reasons for staying together. Mainly it was for Colt, but there were other things, as well. Money, convenience, image. All the excuses people give to themselves when they put up with more than they should because they just can't break the ties that bind them."

She'd forgotten she'd placed her hand over his until her fingers instinctively tightened. She could feel the tension in him. And because she couldn't bring herself to stop his words, she moved her hand under his arm to hold him close. Both for Dylan because he looked as though he needed that contact to get through whatever he was about to tell her, and for herself because she needed an anchor. The balance between them was shifting with every word he uttered, and she knew it was no small thing for him to tell her what happened. How she felt about it happening, she wasn't so sure.

"I knew Lauren was upset and getting angrier with every day that passed, so I decided to placate her and fly home long enough to check on her and Colt before flying out the next morning." A rough huff left his chest. "I was prepared to give her about eight hours of my life. I thought, given our situation, that was enough, but all I really wanted was to see my son."

She'd wondered if Dylan's marriage was a happy one. Now she knew. But knowing it had ended badly, and in tragedy, wasn't a good feeling. Who could be happy about that?

"When I got there the house was already in flames. I was so exhausted I remember just sitting there in the driveway because I thought I'd fallen asleep. I thought I was having a nightmare."

"No one goes home expecting to see that. You were probably in shock."

"All I could think about was Colt. I wasn't even sure he was there. Sometimes Lauren left him with a cousin of hers but I had to know for sure. The front of the house was impassable so I ran around to the back to find a way in."

"Dylan." She smoothed her hand over his arm again, unable to imagine carrying that night not only in his mind but on his body. "If the memories are too much, you don't have to continue."

"Yes, I do."

His head swung toward her and Alex was taken aback by the urgent, almost desperate need she saw in his eyes. As though he wanted to tell her, *had* to tell her.

"All I've thought about today is kissing you again, being with you. And even though I'd rather never talk about the fire again, you need to know this about me first."

Being with her? As in *sleep* with her?

What do you think he means?

Wondering if she'd lost her mind because she didn't *do* casual sex, she went over the rest of his words. What did she have to know about him? "Tell me."

"I broke Colt's window and climbed in. Colt wasn't in his bed and I thought he wasn't there so I went to the bedroom door to get to Lauren." He closed his eyes, squeezing them tight. "I almost missed him, I wouldn't have seen Colt at all if I hadn't tripped over him."

Oh, dear God. Colt was in the fire, too? "But you found him," she whispered, hoping to soothe him, remind him, well able to imagine the thoughts in Dylan's head right now. "And he's fine. Was he conscious?"

Dylan nodded. "He was crying. He had his hands over his ears and he—he kept saying, 'Mommy.'"

"What did you do?"

"The flames were coming under his door, right next to where we were. I didn't think, I just grabbed the first thing I could and tried to put them out so we could get out of there. So I could get Colt out." He swallowed, and took a deep, ragged breath. "There was this sound...this horrible noise. I didn't realize what it was."

She waited for him to continue, dread heavy in her stomach.

"Lauren was screaming. I think that's what Colt heard, why he had his hands over his ears and was sitting there by the door, like he was waiting for her."

Alex gasped, her free hand shooting to her mouth to cover it. She burrowed into Dylan's side, her head on his shoulder, taking comfort as much as she offered it. She said a prayer for Dylan's wife because it was the only thing she could do, and tightened her hold on Dylan. What a horrible way to die. What a horrible thing to *hear*. She couldn't fathom the pain and terror they had all endured.

"I took Colt out the window. I had to get him out but I thought I had enough time. I thought I could get to them from the outside."

All of the pain missing from Dylan's voice the afternoon he'd said Colt's mother was dead was present now. She heard it, felt it. Saw it on his face. But when his words repeated in her head, she frowned. *Them?* "Was someone else there?"

There was no mistaking his expression now. Such a bitter twist to his lips.

"Lauren wasn't alone. Her boyfriend's car was in the driveway. He was in the bedroom with her."

Her *boyfriend?* With Colt in the same house with them?

"I got Colt away from the house but the roof caved in. That's when she stopped screaming."

Alex sat there in stunned silence, unable to feel much of anything except horror for all Dylan and Colt had been through.

"Alexandra, I swear to you I was going back, I was going back to try to save them but I had to get Colt out. I had to make sure he was somewhere safe so he wouldn't follow me."

"Of course. Why would you—?" Suddenly she knew. People talked. Said cruel things.

"I wasted precious seconds sitting in the driveway staring at the flames."

No. She could hear a lot of things and keep her mouth closed, but she couldn't handle that. "Dylan, you're an intelligent man. That was shock setting in. Who wouldn't be completely caught off guard and *terrified* at coming home and seeing that? Knowing your family was inside?" She lifted her hand to his face and gently angled it toward her. So close, she could see the little lines around his eyes. "Everyone thinks of things they should've said or *done* after they lose someone. It's natural."

Dylan stared into her eyes and she felt the connection all the way to her soul. His hazel gaze was a turbulent sea of wariness and disbelief, reluctance that seemed to turn to thankfulness? Maybe hope?

"You don't think I should've done more? That there isn't a chance I hesitated because I knew what she'd been doing with him?"

Is that what he thought? What others had thought *of* him? That he'd left his wife and lover inside on purpose, because Lauren was with another man? "No, I don't."

"How can you be sure?"

How could she explain her instinct? Her sense of self-preservation and intuition? Whatever the name, she knew the truth. Dylan was so shaken by tragedy, he'd lost all objectivity but she knew. "Because even though I'm sure you were angry at them for what they were doing with your son in your home, you aren't a sociopath capable of hurting someone that way. Did you call 911?"

"Someone else did. There wasn't time."

"Which means you put their safety above your own," she pointed out, "because if you'd put yourself first you would've made that call and waited for the fire department to arrive. You wouldn't have gone inside a burning house after them."

Holding him close, she closed her eyes, her forehead against his jaw, trying to think of a way to reach him. Given the newness of their…relationship or friendship or whatever it was, was she crazy to feel so sure?

Alex went over what he'd told her and tried to think of it in ways a man might. Then she knew *why* he'd told her. Why he'd said she had to know before anything else happened between them like kissing or—*being* together.

Dylan was afraid she'd believe the worst and he was giving her an out.

Was that why he'd ended things so abruptly last night? Why he'd kept his distance today?

Maybe what he'd told her should make a difference but it didn't. His past was more than she'd wanted to encounter on her trip to Alaska, but no man could fake the look Dylan wore, could fake being as tormented as he was. And she didn't believe he'd told her anything but the truth. "Did you expect me to think you're a murderer?" she asked softly, her heart pounding in her chest because she knew by the shifting and lowering of his gaze that she was right.

"Some people do."

"Not me. Dylan, I look at your face and I see the truth." She lifted her hand and smoothed a finger over his jaw, his beard soft to the touch. "Who blames you? Lauren's family?"

"She didn't have much family but they weren't the only ones who thought it suspicious under the circumstances."

Because of the other man in Lauren's bedroom. "Okay, fine. You didn't get them out. But what about the man she was with? Why didn't *he* get them out? What about Lauren? She was an adult. Why didn't *she* save Colt and get them out before the fire spread?"

Who knew what anyone's response would be in that type of situation? As much as she'd like to think she would run into a burning building to save her family, it was as likely that she would freeze, so horrified by what was happening that she couldn't move.

The thought didn't sit well. For all her worldly travels and adventures, it was a humbling realization to discover that cowardliness about oneself.

"According to the autopsies both of them had been drinking pretty heavily. I didn't hear the man with her screaming, only her."

No wonder the fire had gotten so out of hand without anyone discovering it. "Dylan, I can only imagine the pain you feel given all you've endured. I hate that you and Colt have gone through such a thing, but all I *see* when I look at you? All I see is a man who risked everything to save his family. Colt was a *baby* and your priority in getting him out first was right on the mark. You might have been angry at your wife but did you *want* her to die?"

"No."

His whisper was strong, adamant.

"Regardless of who she was with, she was Colt's mother and she was a good one."

He praised Lauren, even after her betrayal. "Then make every moment you have with Colt count even more because his mother isn't here to share them with him. Leave the past where it belongs—in the past."

The gratitude and warmth in his eyes gave away his intent to kiss her. They were side by side, nearly nose to nose. Then his mouth was on hers and she was in his arms. This kiss was desperate and thankful and hotter than any they'd shared last night. It was a kiss of life and hope, and she was so glad to share it with him.

When Dylan finally let her up for air, he kept her close, his breath hitting her mouth.

"We pick the worst damn places to do this."

She laughed, still trying to catch her breath from the fierceness of the kiss and agreeing completely. She didn't know what would happen between now and Saturday when it was time for her to leave Deadwood Mountain, but for the first time ever she knew she was getting involved with someone associated with the business being reviewed.

"You're cold again. And hungry from the sounds of your stomach."

Alex laughed, embarrassed. "I am. And Zeke and the others probably ate lunch with their faces pressed against the window watching for us. Any longer and they'll be sending out a search party."

"We'd better go back."

"Yes."

But neither of them wanted to go. They didn't move.

Then she had a thought, crazy as it sounded. "Dylan, what if...I have a proposition for you?"

Dylan raised a thick eyebrow and dropped a chaste kiss on her forehead. "You've definitely got me curious."

She fingered the zipper of his coat, suddenly nervous because she'd never really propositioned a guy before. Stumbling and rambling her way through an explanation about her canceled tours, she finally shut up and simply asked, "So, would you be interested in spending more time with me?"

Oh, what a question, such a hard question to ask. What if after everything he said no?

"I've never been anyone's tour guide. I know Alaska's history pretty well because it's something I'm interested in, but that's about it."

"If you'd rather not take it on right now, I understand. You have your hands full with Colt and running the lodge."

He winced at her words.

"What? Did something happen?"

Dylan wrapped his arms around her and snuggled her close. "I got into it with Zeke again this morning. I'm definitely going to check into buying that land I told you about."

Good. He was making plans, putting the past behind him the way she'd urged him to do. The way he needed to do.

"But I'm definitely interested. Alexandra, you don't have any doubts? Any reservations?"

About the fire, about him, about *being* with him. That's what he meant. She gave him a soft, lingering kiss. "Does that answer your question?"

"I do like the thought of your cold nose pressed against my cheek for two more weeks."

Alex watched as he gave her an oh, so slow and gorgeously sexy smile.

"If you're sure, I guess you have a tour guide."

CHAPTER TEN

ALEX DOWNED HER LUNCH, ignored Zeke, Ansel and Walter's questioning, inquisitive stares, then claimed fatigue the moment Dylan left to do some work he needed to do.

Dylan obviously had reservations about whatever was happening between them—with good reason after the betrayal of his past and what had been said—and so did she. But another worry was her credibility.

She had to write the review. She needed to get it out of the way, so when her vacation began she'd be completely free to enjoy her time with Dylan. His reaction to her being a reviewer was no longer a worry, now that she knew he planned to leave Zeke's lodge, anyway.

Safely ensconced in her room, Alex stared at the screen of her laptop and reread what she'd written so far.

Deadwood Mountain Lodge's location along Chakachama Lake is a nature lover's paradise. Try a walk along the paths surrounding the rustic lodge, or sit on the dock and let your feet dangle over the edge as you practice your casting skills. Fly-fishing is a must-try for every traveler. Even this novice managed to catch the fish of the day and basked in the glow of a bonfire after being stuffed full of arctic char grilled to perfection.

She inserted the photos she'd taken the day after her arrival, then saved the document. With work—and the lingering ethical dilemma—nominally satisfied, memories of Dylan's kisses took over and her body warmed. Her mind whirled in a totally hot-for-her-host kind of way but she didn't know what to *do* about it given that she only had *two weeks*.

Why kiss him? Why start *anything* with him when she knew their time together would be so brief?

Because this has been the most romantic few days of your life?

It was true. Of all the places she'd traveled, of all the men she'd shared drinks with, danced with or flirted with, the time she'd spent with Dylan *had* been the most romantic. Last night on the dock beneath the northern lights, today on the boat….

She felt the connection building, but all too soon she would have to fly to Anchorage, return to work reviewing whatever hotel or resort David was sending her to in Cabo. And go home to Tennessee and face her family at Christmas knowing they were upset that she'd blown them off to spend Thanksgiving in Alaska.

With Dylan.

Just like that, her thoughts made a complete circle in her head and she was back to her original question. Could she handle something so casual? She could count her lovers on one hand and have a finger or two left.

Extending her stay at Deadwood Mountain when she

sensed what would undoubtedly happen between her and Dylan was self-indulgent, even irresponsible.

But it will be fun.

Yes. Totally fun. Still, toss in the fact they knew little about each other and the crazy measure shot to ginormous proportions. Sure, he'd shared some about his past and her heart broke for him, but what woman in this day and age shared *anything* with a guy without first checking him out online? Amazing what you could discover about a person by typing their name into a few sites on the Internet.

At the same time, what if she shut Dylan down, walked away, and always wondered?

What if she and Dylan really had *it,* that magical, mystical quality some couples had, and she left on Saturday when she should be screaming, "Yes, yes, yes!"

She wanted to scream.

Wanna knock some boots, do ya?

No. Well, yes, okay, she did, but *no*. She wasn't raised to do these types of things. The suddenness of it would make her feel cheap and easy and yet already she felt more for Dylan than she had for past boyfriends she'd dated longer.

After watching her parents' and grandparents' marriages over the years, however, she knew she was a true romantic. She *believed* in commitment. At the very least she felt a person should get to know someone and form an emotional connection *before* muddying the waters with sex.

Haven't you formed that connection already? And who says you're going to do anything?

She dropped her head back against the headboard.

It's two weeks of sightseeing and touring and friendship. Companionship. No other decisions have been made.

True. But what about the big question. What if being with Dylan was wonderful? What if they did hook up? Then what? She loved her job, her *life*, exactly as it was right now.

You're the one who made the offer.

Yes. Yes, she had and she wanted to stay, wanted Dylan to be her guide for the next two weeks. But she knew exactly where those kisses they'd exchanged could lead. Would she be better off *not* exploring whatever this was between them? Safer? Smarter?

Truthfully, if something did happen, it would be a fling. A two-week, let's have fun, casual *thing*. What else *but* sex could she and Dylan have under the circumstances and time constraints?

This was why people stayed single. All the questions and problems and stress? It was too complicated to *be* with someone.

She shook off her worries and focused on the computer because she wasn't capable of answering questions that hadn't yet become problems. First things first. She had to write the review.

Picking up where she'd left off, she typed:

The brochure doesn't lie. The rustic lodge is 2,600 square feet of plank pine floors worn to a golden sheen, shared bathroom facilities that are clean but plain, and breathtaking views. Basic meals prepared by Zeke, a fabulous host who values bulk and sustenance over presentation. No five-star cuisine here, just simple, good-tasting fare: caribou stew with fresh-baked corn bread, moose steak with baked potatoes or, my favorite, fresh-caught fish grilled over a fire with bean soup, corn bread and Zeke's chocolate cake for dessert.

Alex added the photos she'd taken of her arctic char, the filleting process and a shot of it on the mesh being cooked over the flames for David to select from and approve.

Getting into the groove, she hunted through the many photos she'd taken to find just the right ones, and gave herself over to pointing out the best features of the lodge. But once that was done and her many photos attached, she came to the difficult part—being honest about where the destination fell short.

My main complaints regarding this establishment would be the means of transportation—i.e., *very* small plane—and the lack of Internet and phone access. This is not a place to conduct business, and I'd be worried if faced with an emergency due to the remote location. The lack of outside contact is definitely something to keep in mind if you suffer from a medical condition of any sort.

She went on to list the lack of electricity after ten, the shared bathrooms and a few other little things she'd noticed during her stay.

By now you're wondering if this tropical heat-loving girl would return to Deadwood

Mountain Lodge. My answer? Yes. Without hesitation. The owner and his guides are informative, friendly and attentive hosts who will show travelers *their* Alaska. Not a tourist-filled street filled with shops and restaurants but the beauty of the earth the way it was intended to be. Rating: 4 stars.

Here she added the photographs she'd taken from the other side of the lake featuring the lodge with the mountain range towering into the sky, the red-and-white plane floating by the pier, the one-room cabins and the green truck parked by the toolshed. She also included photos of the northern lights, the dead trees poking out of the lake and the bear fishing, the eagles soaring overhead and the ducks on their journey south.

If David used half the photos, the two-page spread would be full and it would go a long way to promoting Zeke's lodge.

Alex saved the review on her hard drive and flash drive before exiting the program, knowing the document still needed to be tweaked but allowing herself time to mull over any additions or changes. A rating of four out of five was good, maybe too good. She had to be fair and that might mean taking it down to three-point-five due to the not shabby but older furnishings, the lack of private baths, et cetera. Again, something she could decide later now that the bulk was completed.

She closed the laptop slowly, her heart picking up speed. She'd tweak the review during her last two days at the lodge, and e-mail it to her boss the next time she had Internet access. But now there was nothing standing in the way of whatever happened next between her and Dylan.

The question was—what did she want to happen?

AFTER LUNCH DYLAN HAD excused himself and spent a couple hours chopping wood and a couple more switching out the Super Cub's floats to wheel-skis. The process required using the tractor to lift the two-passenger plane out of the water, making the change, double-checking it, then readying it for flight.

The entire time he replayed the conversation with Alexandra, searching his mind for any signs of hesitation or disbelief on her part.

Truth was he looked forward to the upcoming two weeks with more enthusiasm and anticipation than he'd ever thought possible. Because if Alexandra stayed as warm and forgiving and *genuine* as she appeared…

He smelled dinner the moment he walked into the utility room. Alexandra's laughter drifted to him, light and sweet, along with the deep voices of the older men. She'd mentioned downloading her photos and getting some work done. Given her mood after the heaviness of their discussion, he figured she must have made headway.

After washing his hands, Dylan stepped through the opening between the rooms, unprepared for the kick in the chest he received when he spotted Alexandra noticing Colt's chin dripping in spaghetti sauce. Smiling, she leaned over and gently wiped Colt's face with a napkin. Such a simple gesture, but it was also packed full of tenderness and caring. Colt went right back to eating but Dylan knew by the look on Alexandra's face as she watched Colt that she was thinking of the fire, imagining him not sitting there right now.

He looked at Alexandra from beneath his long thick lashes, a shy smile curling his lips. The sauce was back on his chin, maybe deliberately so? Laughing, Alexandra wiped his face again. And Colt let her.

Looked as though Dylan wasn't the only one curious about their guest.

ONCE DINNER WAS OVER and the dishes cleaned in a group effort, everyone settled in the living room. By request Dylan got his guitar and strummed a few tunes but often he found himself looking at Alexandra as she showed the others some of her photos. And no wonder.

Her whole face lit up when she smiled, and she had a sparkle in her lavender eyes that couldn't be diminished. She laughed a lot, and enjoyed her life. And it showed.

"Hey, stop. Go back. That was a good one of me catching that lake trout. Ansel, come look at this. You should see this. She got that moose we saw the other day." Walter pointed a finger at the screen. "Could I get a copy of that one?"

Shaking her head with yet another laugh, Alexandra shifted her position on the hard wooden seat of the dining chair, the click of the laptop's mouse and keyboard blending in with the snap and crackle of the fire burning in the grate. "Sure. I'll add it to the other ones you want."

Walter didn't seem to get that her photos were to be sold, not given away, but Alexandra didn't seem to mind. She had a soft spot for both Walter and Ansel, teasing them as much as she was teased.

Zeke was right. His first impression of Alexandra had been skewed by his past experiences. Alexandra might possess Lauren's flair for fashion but she was nothing like Lauren otherwise.

Drawn, Dylan set the guitar aside and moved closer to see her computer screen and the slide show of photos. There were a few shots of Ansel and Walter enjoying the scenery, but none of him or Colt that he saw.

In the scheme of things, it probably wouldn't matter if she photographed them. He and Colt had changed a lot since he'd moved them from California. Anyone who knew him then would be hard-pressed to recognize him now. Before he'd been clean shaven, his hair shorter and expertly styled away from his face, his clothes expensive. But the biggest change of all was how he and Colt had both aged. Colt no longer looked like a toddler but like a little boy. As for himself, well, it was amazing what a beard and two years of hell could do to a man. He looked ten years older than he was and definitely sported a lot more wrinkles and gray hair.

"I almost forgot," Alexandra said when the show ended. With quick, efficient movements, she shut the computer down. "I've been meaning to ask where Colt's cabin and corral came from. The set is beautifully carved. I'd love to get one for my nephew for Christmas."

Dylan glanced toward the toys she referred to. "Those were a gift from one of the local families."

"It was a thank-you," Zeke added. "Storm was headed our way but the family had a medical emergency. No one else would risk flying out but Dylan jumped in his plane and answered their distress call. He flew them to Anchorage to the hospital and saved their little girl. Doc said fifteen more minutes and her appendix would've ruptured."

Dylan felt Alexandra staring at him and had to make himself meet her gaze, her words from that afternoon repeating in his head. He knew he'd have done everything he could to rescue Lauren and her lover but when the world turned against him, doubts had crept in. As to the Foxx's little girl... "I was the closest, that's all. Owen Foxx carves the sets to sell in the craft stores and galleries in Anchorage and Fairbanks."

"No need for her to get them there when you've agreed to be her guide. You can take her to meet Owen himself," Zeke stated. "Alex would probably like his workshop."

Alexandra gave Dylan a sheepish glance. "I hope you don't mind. I told them you've agreed to be my guide. I wanted to make sure Zeke didn't rent my room."

"And like I told Alex," Zeke said, nodding at Dylan. "There's no need for either one of you to worry about leaving Colt with me. This late in the season it's slow and Ansel and Walt have decided to stay on a while longer, too. They said they'd help me keep an eye on the boy while you're showing Alex around. When Sam brings the hunters in tomorrow I'll talk to him about flying them back to Anchorage on Saturday while you flight-see with Alex."

It was a perfect plan. Almost too perfect? Either Zeke was trying to matchmake, which he no doubt was, or— "You're not trying to convince Ansel to sign off on your physical, are you? It wouldn't be legal since he's retired."

Ansel and Walter chuckled while Alexandra shot Zeke a look of concern.

"He was. But I've already talked to Zeke about the dangers of him flying alone," Ansel murmured.

"You people sure know how to ruin a man's mood. And that's enough said about me never getting to fly solo again." Zeke added a glare to back up his complaint.

"But you'll get to fly with a copilot able to take over for you if you get into trouble, and that's all that matters, right?" Ansel lowered himself into the recliner and popped the footrest up. To Dylan he said, "Walt and I had talked about flying home through Montana and spending a few days wandering around there but given Zeke's invitation we figured we might stay on since we're enjoying ourselves so much. Might even spend Thanksgiving if we don't wear out our welcome."

The words reminded Dylan about the argument he'd had with Zeke. Given Alexandra's response to his past, he was reluctant to think beyond the next two weeks. Why get his hopes up when Zeke was wrong about being able to have a life?

There was certainly a lot more to tell Alexandra, but only time would tell whether or not he felt she could handle the reality of his identity. And God only knew if anyone could be trusted with the secret burden he carried.

Wasn't it enough that Alexandra knew about the fire? Did the rest really matter if she believed him?

"So we can go there?" Alexandra asked. "Add the workshop to the tours? We haven't exactly discussed all the details and stops I had scheduled but I'd love to see this place."

"It's not a problem. I'll take you." The moment the words left Dylan's mouth, a scene popped into his head, this one more defined than the previous.

"Well, now that's a problem. I could take you to Frisco with me but it'll cost you."

"How much?"

"A thousand dollars."

"What? That's preposterous!"

Jesse grabbed the woman by the waist and hauled her off his horse. The moment her feet touched solid ground, he swung himself into the saddle.

Evangeline Taylor from Boston, Massachusetts, was a pain in the ass.

He'd listened to her whine and complain the entire five miles to town, and he wouldn't cart her to San Francisco without being well compensated for it, especially since he couldn't gag her. "You want to get there in one piece or take your chances with a man who tried to flip your skirts the moment you were out of screamin' range?"

"Ain't that right, Dylan?"

Zeke's voice cut into the fog. Dylan blinked to awareness, embarrassed to realize he'd been staring blankly at Alexandra while the setting details and dialogue filled his head in rapid succession.

Not a full scene, but it was more than he'd had in over two years.

"Dylan, are you feeling okay?" Alexandra asked.

"I'm fine. Just distracted," he said.

Like it or not, he realized a fictional heroine was taking shape in his head. And Evangeline Taylor smelled like spice, had lavender-colored eyes and a proud chin that stuck up in the air and taunted the gunslinger-turned-adventurer about to take her on the ride of her life. To San Francisco. No, the Klondike. San Francisco would only be the first stop.

In all the books he'd published, he'd never written about the Klondike and after two years of living here and researching Alaska's history, it would be perfect.... But how could he even consider the prospect? For his own entertainment? Something to ease the boredom of winter while he planned his house?

He'd always found the process of writing fun, very much like a puzzle that had to be put together. The scene was a piece, one of many that might eventually make up a story.

"I told Alex you two should get a good idea of tours and prices and such. The loft is free and quiet."

Dylan ran a hand over his face in an attempt to banish the scene from his mind. He hadn't written a word in a very long time. Writing, like his life in California, belonged to his past.

Alexandra studied him, a frown furrowing her brow. "Are you *sure* you're feeling okay? We can do it tomorrow if you'd like."

And give up part of the short time he had to spend with her? Dylan tilted his head toward the stairs, grateful for once that Zeke had interfered. "First door at the top of the stairs."

CHAPTER ELEVEN

DYLAN WATCHED THE TANTALIZING sway of Alexandra's backside as she walked to the double windows fronting the miniscule room. No auroras tonight.

He perched himself on the edge of the desk. "What did you have lined up to see?"

Alexandra shot him a look over her shoulder, her eyes full of questions.

"I'm fine," he said in response. "I didn't sleep much after what happened on the dock because I felt I needed to talk to you. It's catching up to me. Now tell me what you want to see."

She gave him a sweet smile. "Everything? I realize now I was overly optimistic in how much I had planned. When I travel I like to see as much of the area as possible because I usually never visit the same place—"

It wasn't hard to finish her sentence. "You never visit the same place twice?"

"Yeah."

It was a reminder that she wasn't staying, a reminder of where they stood with each other.

"So, anyway, I'd like to see the glaciers. I've heard they're awesome. And Mount Redoubt and Spur up close. I'd love to photograph one of the abandoned mining towns you and Zeke have told us about, Owen Foxx's, of course, and wolves if possible but I know that's a stretch. Oh, and the hot springs and the Kenai Peninsula. I thought my last two days could be spent touring Anchorage," she continued in a nervous rush. "It probably comes as a surprise, but I like to shop."

"Really?" He didn't think he'd ever met a woman who didn't like to shop. But her words made him leery. Did she want him to show her around Anchorage? Taxiing up to the small airport gate to pick up Zeke's passengers was one thing. But spending days walking amongst crowds of tourists, people in general, was his idea of hell.

"Yeah. There were some nice-looking galleries and shops online. I'd like to visit them in person."

A flight plan began to form in his head as well as a calendar of things he already had scheduled. "I can fly you to Anchorage at the end of your stay but I may not be able to show you around it or the peninsula. You'll be able to rent a car and drive, though. No problem."

"Oh."

Was she disappointed? Hadn't she just reminded him she couldn't stay? "How about I put together an itinerary based on what you've said and we go from there? Some of the areas you've named are on the route for supply drops. I've been filling in for Zeke since his heart attack but if you can handle a few extra takeoffs and landings, you could go with me."

She made a face at the mention of flying but then her shoulders squared. "I can do that. I knew I had to fly small when I booked but I swear the planes looked so much bigger on the Internet. I'll be fine, though, really. Just don't get mad and toss me out of the plane if I hurl."

"It's happened before."

A burst of laughter escaped her and she sent him a wary glance. "The hurling? Or throwing the hurler out of the plane?"

He smiled at her joke, liked that she felt comfortable with him. "Guess we'll have to find out."

Hearing voices, Dylan glanced toward the open door as Ansel and Walter drifted by. Both men glanced inside, their hopeful expressions easy to read.

Dylan glanced at his watch. He'd put Colt to bed at eight. Zeke had probably gone to his room, too, and now the house was quiet, the generator on for only a few more minutes. He should let her go so she could get ready for bed while they still had lights.

"Dylan, about today."

Unease flooded him. She'd had time to think over his confession. Were doubts kicking in? Was she reconsidering the attraction between them? "I can fly you and keep my hands to myself." It would be hell now that he'd tasted her and wanted more, but he'd do it.

Her expression softened. "Dylan." She stepped in front of him, resting her hands on his arms. "It's not that. I don't want to send you mixed signals, that's all."

Mixed signals? "What do you mean?"

She pulled one of his hands off the edge of the desk where he gripped it, and carried it to her mouth. She'd said his scars didn't bother her but they bothered him. His hands were bare and the sight of his mottled skin was wrong against the smoothness of her face and lips. His chest seized when she kissed his knuckles and opened his palm to hold it to her cheek.

"I'm glad you were honest with me today and you

told me what happened. And I haven't changed my mind. I can see who you are. But I am feeling a little freaked out by how fast things are moving and I thought if I'm feeling this way, maybe you are, too?"

He managed a nod, not sure what to say. Not sure what he felt besides humbled and turned on and in over his head because he'd never thought he'd feel this way again.

"I don't want you to get the wrong idea about me," she said. "I'm decisive and independent, and I *love* my freedom. But those kisses were…" She shook her head, as if at a loss to express what she meant.

Mind-blowing? Seductive? "Powerful?" he suggested.

"Yes." She closed her eyes briefly. "And after kissing you and agreeing to spend the next two weeks with you, even though I *want* to explore what's happening between us, I need time. You might think I'm a tease for saying this now, but when you kiss me I forget common sense and morals and time frames and…I don't want to make a mistake."

"What are you saying, sweetheart?"

A visible battle took place across the angles and planes of her face. "I'm saying," she whispered, her voice firm, "that no matter how powerful those kisses are, I'm *not* making any promises to sleep with you because I haven't even known you a week. So bottom line—" she took a deep breath "—no pressure, no promises when it comes to whatever happens between us. Okay?"

Sometimes he wondered if she could read his mind.

Dylan used his hold on her to tug her to him and brush his lips over her mouth. She shivered.

Seeing her physical response, the way her eyes

darkened to a smoky-blue, his hands shook when he gathered her closer, between his sprawled legs.

When their bodies made full contact Dylan kissed her again, softly, keeping the kiss light and tasting her warmth, lingering over the caress because he knew it was all he'd get, all either of them could handle. For now.

As he ended the kiss he noted the way the pulse at her throat raced. "Whatever you want."

THE NEXT DAY ALEX MEANDERED into the quiet lodge, her thoughts on Dylan and their agreement.

Ansel and Walter were fishing. She'd chatted with them briefly and taken pictures of a bear with her long range zoom lens as it drank across the lake, but she had no desire to stand in the cold water. Hiking didn't appeal, either.

After Dylan had kissed her good-night in the loft, she'd descended the stairs on wobbly legs.

Her grandmother was a firm believer that things happened for a reason and that troubles, heartache and even good times played out in life as they were meant to. Gram believed that all things work for good to those who believed. Now Alex had to find that faith and shove her insecurities aside. What else could she do?

Pausing in front of one of the windows, she looked out at the sound of a plane approaching, slowing to make that terrifying water landing. Experiencing it from the air had been horrible but watching the smooth, easy glide of the plane as the floats connected with the water wasn't bad at all. From this angle, there was a grace to the motion, a mechanical version of the ducks she'd seen earlier.

So maybe to get through her future landings, she needed to focus on the positive. Picture the successful landing in her mind.

Couldn't hurt.

The green truck appeared from the road leading to the cabins and she saw Dylan making his way down the slope to the dock. Dylan arrived before the plane floated into position and when he got out he said something to Ansel and Walter that had all three of them laughing.

Dylan leaned against the truck in a casual pose, and she narrowed her gaze to take in his handsome profile, the way the breeze ruffled his hair and the collar of his coat. She'd kissed that neck. She could taste him now if she closed her eyes and—

"Awfully pretty day to be holed up in here," Zeke said from behind her.

Alex jumped, heat filling her cheeks because of her thoughts. How long had he been watching her? And with that peculiar gleam in his eyes? She forced a smile to her lips and hoped he didn't notice her heightened color. "I've been out for a walk."

"Must not have gone too far if you're back already. You feeling okay? You missed breakfast and you're looking a little flushed."

So much for not noticing. "I'm fine. Too many layers," she said, plucking at her turtleneck. Going one step further to prove her point, she shrugged off her thermal-insulated vest. "And I wasn't hungry this morning, so I worked for a while." She'd made another pass through her review and added a few things, removed a few sentences. And dropped the rating to three and a half stars. She felt bad about that but beauty didn't make up for the lack of amenities and readers of *Traveling Single* expected certain things from a four star rating.

"You work too much. You're on vacation, remember? Something happen last night with Dylan that you're staying in here to avoid him?"

Alex stilled. Gentle, well-intended matchmaking was one thing, but everyone in the house offering advice and psychoanalysis? That was uncomfortable to say the least. "I don't know what you mean. Nothing happened. We just talked about my tours."

Zeke turned and muttered something under his breath. Something like...*stupid boy?*

Sensing her chance to ask questions and get answers without putting Dylan on the spot and making him relive a nightmare, Alex followed Zeke into the kitchen and made her way to the counter where the coffeepot sat. "Zeke, are you sure you're okay with Dylan taking me on those tours?"

"Absolutely," Zeke said. "Dylan needs a few days away from here to relax and think about things. Showing you the sights would be just the thing."

To relax and think about what things?

Does it matter? You can't expect him to reveal his life history in one big gush.

Besides, did she want him to do that? "Maybe I can help. Is something wrong?"

Zeke's gaze shifted and settled on his grandson. Colt played on the far side of the living room but was visible through the opening between the two rooms. She'd walked right in, over to the window and hadn't even known Colt was there.

As before, Dylan's son played with his carved wooden set. He was in the process of setting up the toys that included fencing, several cows, horses, dogs and even a few cowboys.

Her gaze on Colt, her mind blanked when she saw Colt's mouth move as though the cowboy in his hand talked to his horse. But unlike her nephew Matt, who made all sorts of play sounds and character voices, Colt made no sound at all.

Wait a minute. Had she *ever* heard him speak?

That first day when she'd taken Colt's photograph, Dylan had said Colt suffered emotional issues from his mother's death. Could his silence be one of them? "Zeke, can I ask you something?"

"Suppose that depends on what it is."

"It's not about the stash of cigars I found in the pantry when I was looking for the coffee filters."

Zeke shot her a look that questioned whether or not she'd keep his secret. "I'm doing everything else the docs have said. A man's gotta have some fun."

Alex smiled at his words but tilted her head toward Colt. "I don't mean to pry, but it just dawned on me that I've never heard Colt speak, and I've never heard him respond when spoken to. Is something wrong?" she asked, careful to keep her voice from carrying to where the child played.

Zeke's expression—a mix of wariness and sadness—razored into her soul. "Might be best if you ask Dylan."

So there *was* something wrong. Dylan had told her about his wife, the fire. Why not tell her about Colt? Did he not feel that he could? "He's told me Colt has emotional issues from the fire, but didn't explain what."

"He told you that?" Zeke looked pleased by the news, as though Dylan talking about his son was unusual.

So maybe Zeke would fill in the blanks?

"Surely you know me well enough by now to know I would never do anything to hurt Colt. To hurt anyone," she clarified. "I'm only asking because I'm concerned."

"We're all concerned."

"Colt's problems are serious?" She blinked in confusion. "But I don't understand. If Colt was that traumatized by the fire, why does Dylan have him here? No offense, but why not live somewhere where Colt could receive help and whatever therapy he needs?"

"Like I said, you need to ask Dylan that."

Zeke's tone made her wonder if the subject was a touchy one. She would ask Dylan. In the meantime, she could only imagine the worry Zeke felt for both his son and grandson. She was a stranger and she worried about them. Colt was a shadow instead of the light he should be. How much did he remember about the fire? Hadn't scientists learned fear imprinted images in memory?

Zeke released a heavy sigh and resumed his task of folding dish towels. "I can practically hear the cranks in your head turnin'. So listen 'cause I'll only say this once since Dylan will probably be madder than a goat that I told you. Colt shows no sign of brain damage. He's not autistic and he isn't shy," Zeke informed her softly. "But the truth is, he hasn't spoken a word since his mama died."

Zeke put the towels away, then began pulling out pots and pans and ingredients for lunch. "The docs and shrinks say he'll come out of it in time but so far he hasn't." He started crushing cornflakes he'd put in a plastic bag.

Poor little guy. Her heart broke for Colt. For Dylan and Zeke, too. No wonder Dylan seemed to carry so much guilt. He'd lost more than his home and marriage, troubled though it was. He'd lost the sound of his son's voice. Colt hadn't spoken in *years?*

"Dylan doesn't want people to know Colt doesn't talk. Part of why he's so upset with me for turning this place into a lodge is that he's afraid for Colt's safety with me advertising it and such. So when people come, we just let them think what they like. Dylan believes it's safer for Colt if guests don't know."

It probably was safer. But she couldn't help but be hurt Dylan hadn't told her.

Zeke dumped the crushed flakes into a mixing bowl as the door opened and the three hunters who'd flown to the spike camp stepped in carrying their gear. Colt's head jerked up at the sight of the newcomers and he got to his feet and ran to the kitchen.

Zeke ruffled Colt's hair and hugged him close to his legs when Colt wrapped one arm around Zeke's thigh.

"That cold air get'cha?" Zeke chuckled. "Say, I need to go talk to those fellas for a second. Shouldn't take me more'n five minutes. Would you mind keeping an eye on Colt while I do that?"

She blinked at the request. Dylan had warned her away from his son after she'd taken Colt's picture but surely that didn't apply now? "Sure."

"Colt, you stay with Alex, okay? I'll just be in the other room but I need to talk to those gents."

Colt looked up at her with his big brown eyes and Alex smiled, uncomfortable with the child's stare. "What do you say, Colt? Would you like to help me?"

CHAPTER TWELVE

ZEKE LEFT THE KITCHEN and Alex tried to come up with something funny to say to draw a smile from Colt. Her mind went blank. Would it make Colt uncomfortable if she talked to him? Should she keep working? Why talk if he won't answer?

She was out of her element when it came to kids. Playing with her infant niece and nephews on trips home wasn't enough to clue her in to this situation. "That's a nice cowboy setup you have in there. Do you like horses?"

Colt made eye contact with her briefly but didn't respond, not even a nod or a shrug.

Alex forced another smile. Okay, then. "I have a horse. She's in Tennessee at my parents' house. They take care of her for me."

Again, no answer, though he did seem to be listening and the expression that flickered across his handsome little face said he liked hearing about her horse. So, horses it was.

"Her name is Bandit. She's an Appaloosa and nearly all white, but she has black socks on all four hooves, black spots on her hindquarters and a black stripe over her eyes and ears like a hat a bandit would wear." She pointed to the cornflakes. "Your grandpa left the recipe here for baked fried chicken but it looks like we need a lot more of those. Would you mind crushing them like your grandpa was? Like this," she said, showing him. "Yeah, perfect."

Colt started crushing the cereal with little-boy fascination and single-minded purposefulness, and more questions about Colt's disability piled up in her head as she told Colt about riding Bandit, grooming her and other things she hadn't thought of in quite a while.

Home. Bandit. Her family. Was she going to wake up one day sad that she'd missed out on what was going on there because she was always traveling? She didn't think so. Especially when it kept her under the radar so her mother's focus was on her brothers rather than her.

Still, the wave of homesickness rolling over her surprised her. Talking with Colt was like chatting up her young nephews. And Ansel and Walter and Zeke reminded her of her many uncles, joking and kidding and telling outrageous tales. The lodge held such a sense of warmth and comfort, it was no wonder it made her think of home.

And that made her remember the antsy, can't-wait-to-get-out-of-here feeling she always got when she stayed too long in one place. She didn't feel it yet. But she would.

She knew it was only a matter of time.

ALEXANDRA BECAME MORE NERVOUS about her decision to stay as the last two days of the original weeklong stay drew to a close. So much so she briefly considered packing her bags and going home to Tennessee thereby skipping her vacation, as a punishment.

Why? Because every time Dylan walked into a room,

her heart picked up speed. Every time he brushed his hand against hers, she caught herself wanting to close the distance and weave their fingers together. And when he talked or smiled at or hugged his son? Her heart totally melted into a big glob of goo.

Yup, she was a total sap. Because every one of those little things Dylan did made her want him more. When they came together—she couldn't even think of it as *if* anymore, which freaked her out to the point of bingeing on Zeke's double chocolate cake—they'd be lucky if they made it to a bed. But no pressure, no promises.

She was determined to take things slow even if she'd never felt this intensely about a guy. But was it pure and simple lust, or the beginnings of something bigger?

She didn't know.

In her twenty-eight years she'd had her share of dates and boyfriends but when her nomad ways and constant traveling wore thin, the relationships always fizzled and ended. Still, sex wasn't something she did casually. Her parents were about to celebrate their fortieth anniversary together, so to her sex equated to long-term dating, commitment, marriage.

Staying with Dylan, hiring him as her tour guide, wasn't something she should even consider *doing* given the temptation she felt for him. But no matter the internal lectures and warnings of what might befall her, here she was.

"Want to help me put Colt to bed?"

Alex looked up in surprise. She'd been sitting staring into the flames in the hearth listening to Dylan play his guitar. Now he stood beside the couch holding his sleepy-eyed son in his arms, and even though there was nothing sexier than the sight of Dylan's scarred hands cradling Colt so protectively against his chest, pure, unadulterated fear zipped through her veins.

You could so totally fall for him.

And what would she do if she did?

Her pulse began to race at warp speed. She'd wanted time to connect, to see how she felt about Dylan but she didn't want to *fall* for him. And in a week? That couldn't happen, could it?

She dropped her gaze and made herself focus on Colt's tired form. The little boy had enough problems without adding to the mix. Whatever happened between her and Dylan, she didn't want Colt to be a casualty and the only way to prevent it was to keep her distance. "Actually I think I'm going to turn in, too. I need to charge my equipment for our first tour tomorrow, and I haven't folded my laundry from earlier today…" And she made excuses and by the awareness on Dylan's face, he knew it.

The warmth in his eyes faded. "Have a good night then."

Oh, you can feel the chill in the air now.

Alex hugged her arms around herself and remained on the couch as Dylan carried his son down the hall to his room.

Dylan had been disappointed by her response. Maybe even hurt? Guilt stirred.

She wanted to call out to him, wanted to follow and listen to Dylan while he read Colt a story about Toad's adventures. But she didn't, partly because of the drama presently playing out in Tennessee. Not long ago her brother Ethan had come home from his sojourn to Niger with Doctors Without Borders with a child in tow. He'd hired their sister-in-law's sister, Megan, to be the boy's nanny. But Megan's habit of messing around, not sticking around, had some members of the family worried.

And like it or not, those same concerns also applied to her. Liking Dylan was one thing, spending time with him and enjoying his company to the fullest extent of wherever it led all fine and dandy, but they had to be careful around Colt. Didn't Dylan see that?

Colt was too young to understand the complexities of relationships, and he didn't need someone else coming into his already confusing, traumatized life, then walking away. Colt's big dark eyes were too observant, too aware of what was happening around him. Even his inability to speak was proof of that. The trauma of the fire and losing his mother had been too much for Colt's immature coping abilities.

Dylan would thank her later because she'd refused his request, would thank her for protecting Colt.

But the sound of Colt's door closing down the hall?

That made her wish she was on the other side with them.

DYLAN LOWERED COLT TO HIS twin bed then lay down beside his son, torn between being happy Alexandra had refused him and angry that she could so easily say no when *he* hadn't been able to stop himself from making the request.

Colt squirmed against Dylan's side, and with a measure of surprise, he realized Colt was shoving the book at him. Once Colt would have sat motionless. The show of impatience was progress. The shrinks and doctors had said to keep testing Colt in little ways, to deliberately do things to provoke a response instead of catering to Colt's every need as Dylan had when Colt was a toddler. The hope was that Colt would get impatient enough to voice his frustration.

Dylan ignored the book and remained silent, his thoughts on Alexandra. In the past he'd never wanted the guests to notice Colt's muteness, but Alexandra knew. Zeke had told Dylan about Alexandra watching Colt today and all evening she'd been pensive and quiet herself.

Was that why she'd said no? Because he hadn't told her or because she was uncomfortable around Colt now as a result? Did she consider his son damaged? He imagined getting involved with a single father was hard enough, but if the child had issues?

No pressure. If Alexandra couldn't handle it, best to find out now.

Colt shoved the book at him again, and even though Dylan knew he ought to wait for one more impatient shove, he accepted the book with a sigh. "You know, one of these days I'm not going to read to you until you ask me with words."

His son blinked at him, all sad-eyed innocence.

Dylan pulled Colt closer and kissed his curly head. "But not tonight. Where were we?"

THE NEXT DAY ALEX FELT the intensity of a stare and turned to find Colt regarding her, his precious face seemingly questioning her preoccupied mood as though debating whether or not to approach her. And since she couldn't be mean to the little boy… "Hey, sweetie. You caught me daydreaming. What's up?"

The boy's arm came out from behind him and he held something out for her to see. A horse?

His favorite, one of the hand-carved horses from the play set she so admired. What did she say to that? "You want me to have it? Keep it?"

His eyes widened in obvious alarm.

"Oh, I couldn't do that." She rushed to assure him. "I can see how much it means to you." So what did he want her to do? Play?

Oh, honey. How am I supposed to say no to you? Especially when she knew he had to be lonely. "I don't know. I was just getting ready to… You know, I suppose I have some free time. Would you mind if I played with the horse? I'll give it back to you when we're done."

Colt gave her a slight nod. Wait a minute—*a nod?* She knew from watching Colt with his father and grandfather that Colt typically didn't respond. At all. "So that's what you want? For me to play with you?"

Wariness settled over his features now, as though he was afraid she would turn him down, afraid she expected him to answer or nod again.

She thought of Bandit, how skittish the mare had been when she'd become part of their family. Her grandfather had been adamant that Alex take things slow, build trust with the animal.

Showing him none of the hesitation she felt, Alex smiled. "I sure miss Bandit. May I name this horse Bandit? Just for today?"

His little shoulders lowered a tad, his tension lessening. He nodded again.

And just like that she understood what her mother meant whenever she became frustrated with Alex's take on marriage and children and freedom. She'd vowed Alex's maternal instincts would kick in one day.

Well, surprise, here they were.

She felt a sense of tenderness and pride, hope and heartache. Sure, Colt had a long way to go but he was making progress right in front of her. Of course, she soon wouldn't be around to see what else he accomplished.

Colt wasn't her child but that nod, that sweet smile after a week of seeing his sad face? Those were hers to cherish and she always would.

And that pragmatic, cynical voice in her head whispered that maybe she'd subconsciously chosen to care for a guilt-ridden man and his son because she knew the problems they possessed were a guarantee she *wouldn't* stick around.

ZEKE GRABBED DYLAN AS SOON as he stepped through the door. "Boys, go stow your fishing gear and wash up. Dinner in about thirty minutes. Dylan, come with me. You gotta see this, son."

Curious, Dylan followed his father down the hallway, minding Zeke's orders to be quiet as they approached Colt's room. What he saw inside nearly sent him to his knees.

Colt sat on his rear bent forward over his crossed ankles, a horse in one hand and a cowboy in the other. No surprise there. The surprise came in seeing Alexandra sprawled on her stomach on a pillow, her legs bent at the knees, feet swinging idly in the air above them while she pretended the horse in her hand was avoiding Colt's attempt to round it up.

Playing. They were playing.

Together.

"Been that way for a while now," Zeke whispered. "Haven't seen him like this with anyone. Not even you and me."

Neither had he. Colt played, yes. But he didn't play *with* those around him. He didn't interact. Until now. Until *her.* Instead of being happy that Alexandra had connected in such a way, the fear in his gut spread. He felt like a man standing at the top of a mud slide, knowing he was about to go down and trying desperately to prepare for the rush.

"Isn't that something?" Zeke whispered the question, a smile in his voice. "I hate to see you take her on those tours now. At least you spaced them out some. Wish she could just spend the next couple weeks hanging around here."

So did Dylan. Standing here spying on Colt and Alexandra as they played, Dylan consciously took the first step Zeke had been pushing him to take since Lauren's betrayal and his arrest and the whole debacle with Belinda.

The two weeks hadn't even begun but he knew it wasn't going to be long enough. Colt was getting attached, he liked her, was reaching out to her.

Like father, like son?

He wasn't sure of the answer but Dylan didn't want that connection to end.

The sight before him made him *believe* a future was actually possible.

As though sensing his perusal, Alexandra glanced up. Their gazes met and locked and unable to help himself, he let his eyes flow over her body. When he made eye contact again, a blush bloomed on her cheeks.

"I'll go watch after dinner," Zeke said. "Get on in there," he ordered before hightailing it down the hall.

Dylan hesitated, uncomfortable even though it was his son and his—what? Girlfriend? Soon-to-be lover?

No pressure, no promises.

Alexandra pushed herself to a sitting position and smiled at him. "Would you like to join us? Colt could use a few more horses to round up."

Dylan lowered himself to the floor and picked up one of the horses presently positioned out of the action, his gaze on the beautiful woman beside him.

How could he convince Alexandra to believe in them when his identity was guaranteed to scare her away?

CHAPTER THIRTEEN

ALEXANDRA ENTERED THE KITCHEN intent on getting a drink of water and interrupted Dylan reading. His gaze swept over her, lingering on parts of her that immediately heated and pebbled in response. That thoroughly destroyed her composure. Why was that all it took with him? A single look and she melted?

It was late, the middle of the night. A battery operated lantern sat on the table in front of Dylan, lighting the pages of his book but cloaking the kitchen cabinets in shadows.

"Can't sleep?"

She shook her head, unable to tell him she was so nervous about flying out to deliver supplies with him as soon as the others left in the morning that she'd tossed and turned since going to bed.

She helped herself to a glass, wishing flannel was as sexy on her as it was him and that her hair didn't look like a rat's nest. "What are you reading?"

"Nothing."

She got a glimpse of the child psychology book and sighed. *Nothing* was pretty heavy material. "I forgot to tell you what Colt did today. Well, it might not be anything but you and Zeke both have said Colt never responds and—"

"He spoke?"

Dylan shot off his stool so fast Alex nearly dropped the glass she held. She managed to keep hold of it, but water sloshed over the rim and onto the floor. Dylan plucked the glass from her hands and set it aside.

"What did he say?"

She stared into Dylan's taut features. His hands gripped her shoulders a little too tightly, his eyes blazed with intensity, and she desperately wanted to tell him what he so obviously needed to hear. "I'm sorry. Dylan, no, Colt didn't speak. I didn't mean to imply that he did."

Dylan's disappointment was visible. His grip loosened until his hands fell to his sides. "I should've known better. You're good but you're not a miracle worker."

Did he expect her to be? Because that definitely counted as pressure.

"Alexandra, I'm sorry I didn't tell you about Colt, that you had to find out the way you did."

She liked his ability to apologize. "I understand. Like taking his photo, it's for his safety."

"Yes. But I should have thought to tell you." He ran a hand over his hair in frustration. "It's become so normal I— Dammit, I don't know what to say."

"You don't have to say anything." She reached out to Dylan, placed her hand on his arm. "Today, Colt didn't speak but I asked him a question and he nodded. I thought it was something."

"It is. You're sure he nodded?"

The intensity was back. Unable to stop it, pleasure filled her chest and a smile curved her lips. Dylan looked so thrilled at the news and she was glad to have given him that, at least. "Twice," she said, explaining what had taken place. "I was going to say something earlier but we began playing then it was dinnertime. It slipped my mind. And I wasn't entirely sure it wasn't normal behavior for him."

Dylan's expression of love and hope and a father's desperation tore at her soul. She stepped close and wrapped him in her arms, feeling the play of muscles along his back and the strength with which he held her.

How could this feel so right and be so scary? Finally she broke the silence. "Talk to me," she whispered. "Tell me what the doctors have said. Tell me so I know how to talk to Colt."

Dylan inhaled, his lips grazing her neck. "Before the fire Colt talked. He said simple words and short sentences. Then nothing."

"Not even a nod?"

"Not even a nod."

Pulling away she caressed his cheek. They hadn't known each other long enough to know the details of each other's lives but he responded to her touch. Not in an I-wanna-get-laid kind of way but in a friendship kind of way. An I'm-*into*-you kind of way. That was a powerful feeling. And oh, so sweet. "That means we need to focus on the positive here. Colt nodded at me, he *answered* me, and that means Colt *is* getting better. It's progress, right? It means he's thinking about it in his head. And maybe next time he will say something and I hope when he does," she said softly, "he says it to you."

Dylan closed his eyes as if in fervent prayer and drew her to his chest once more. He was an affectionate man, touching, holding, brushing his hand against hers. She liked it. Liked it when he smoothed his palms up her back, tangled his fingers in her hair. When he used his grip to gently tip her head back and nuzzled his nose with hers.

Dylan dipped his head and his breath sent shivers down her spine when it tickled her ear. "I'm not surprised Colt responds to you. God knows I do."

Heat pooled low in her belly and that sense of rightness returned. She recognized the signs of desire, of intense and serious *like*. There was something else, too. Something bigger than them both. Was she imagining that?

Dylan smelled good, like fresh air and wood smoke. The scents reminded her of fall in Tennessee, and she knew she'd never smell them again and not think of him.

Alex used his chest for balance and rose onto her tiptoes, giving him a lingering kiss, one that left his eyes dark and made her body tingle. A kiss that brought all sorts of thoughts to her head, most of them warnings and reminders, lists of why she liked her life exactly as it was. Freedom, the ability to answer only to herself. No ties, few worries. A good life, the best life. She was perfectly happy. Splendidly content.

But this feeling was *nice*.

A week with Dylan had made her feel strangely adrift. And it made her question her goals, her lifestyle. Her very core and inner self.

Was she happy? Did she have all the things she wanted? Was she content?

The voice inside her head, usually so sarcastic and witty and ready with sharp-tongued quips about all things, was absurdly, strangely silent, leaving her floating in a realm of feeling with no compass to show her the way.

"HAVE I TOLD YOU THAT YOU ARE one incredible man?"

Dylan smiled at the excited tremor he heard in Alexandra's voice. Some women liked jewelry. Some liked flowers. Apparently Alexandra liked wolves.

They were hunkered down behind a stand of trees and brush, lying side by side for warmth beneath the overcast November sky. He'd admit flying in small planes took some getting used to, but she'd handled their short flight north without throwing up before, during or after landing. That was progress and he'd admit to a sense of pride that she'd conquered her fear to that measure. He'd have to remember Alexandra's preference for wheel skis versus water floats in the future.

Dylan bit back a curse. If they *had* a future. Their time together was short, teetering on half-truths and secrets and the length of her vacation. He couldn't let himself get ahead of things when the future would play out in ways he couldn't predict. All he could do was let her get to know him, feel comfortable, so that when— if—he revealed all to her, maybe it wouldn't matter.

But being a realist, he knew the chances of that happening were against him. Odds were they wouldn't be together in a month and he had to remember that and enjoy the moment for what it was.

"This… Dylan, they are *amazing*."

"I thought you might like them," he whispered.

She gave him an insanely seductive smile. "I definitely like them."

Them, or him? He noted the heat and desire in her gaze and his body responded as it always did.

Tempted, Dylan leaned lower and kissed her, lingering over the caress, taking it deeper and teasing her with all the skill he possessed. She tasted like coffee and apples. Sweetness and light.

Across the field one of the wolves barked and yipped. Dylan ended the kiss, pleased to see Alexandra's eyes were unfocused, her expression soft. They shared a smile before returning to watch the wolves playing close to their den.

Alexandra's entire face lit up at the pups' antics. Balancing carefully, barely a breath of sound escaped as her camera caught the wolves in action. They were shy creatures and wary of humans. He'd brought her to one of his favorite spots. He'd discovered it a year ago and kept the location to himself, needing a place to get away from Zeke's well-meaning lectures.

While Alexandra continued to watch through her lens, he carefully set his binoculars aside and studied her. The tip of her nose was Rudolf-red, her hair sticking out from under what she referred to as her "ugly hat." She'd never looked more beautiful.

Sending her to bed last night alone had been hard but he'd forced himself to do it, reminding himself that every minute that passed and every ounce of trust she placed in him was worth the discomfort he felt. Cold showers had become the norm.

Color began to fill his head, his thoughts shifting to the grit of trail dust, the call of crows and the rush of water over the rocks. In his mind he saw a river, Evangeline picking her way across the bank to the water's edge…

"Dylan? Hey, where'd you go?"

Alexandra's voice cut into the scene evolving in his mind. He blinked to find her staring at him, a smile pulling at her lips.

"What were you thinking about so intensely?"

It was the perfect time to tell her the truth. But he couldn't tell her now. He might scare her if he blurted all here in the middle of nowhere when she was completely at his mercy.

Soon, he promised himself. "You," he said simply, because it was the truth.

DYLAN SAT IN THE LOFT and watched the auroras roll over the sky in neon waves. He should go downstairs and wake Alexandra for the show but he couldn't put himself in such close proximity to her and a bed and be held accountable.

His thoughts were filled with images of Alexandra and her smile today at the sight of the wolves, of Alexandra and Colt lying on the floor playing with Colt's ranch set. Of Alexandra, period.

Maybe it would have been better if Alexandra had recognized him right from the start. Then Dylan wouldn't be sitting here brooding over whether or not to tell her when their time together was limited.

The scuffle of a footfall sounded behind him and without turning he knew who it was. Not his father, not Colt. Her. His entire body went on immediate alert.

"You didn't wake me." It was a complaint, filled with hurt rather than anger.

"Just started a few minutes ago. Can't sleep?"

Alexandra wore her flannel pajamas, a throw

wrapped around her shoulders like a cape. There was enough light emitting from the laptop's screen to allow him to see the color that blossomed in her cheeks.

It was easy to read her thoughts because, since her arrival, he'd had those same kinds of dreams.

The computer screen flickered before it went to a screensaver, plunging them into shadows except for the rolling colors outside the window.

"Dylan...is something wrong?"

With us. The words were there, if unspoken. He closed his eyes briefly, forcing himself to travel back to California. He made himself remember when it was the last thing he wanted to do. Lauren had always claimed he didn't open up to her, didn't communicate enough. And that made him think of the things Alexandra needed to know.

Instantly the fear came and he shot out of the chair, grazing his hand against the mouse in the process. The move was enough that the computer screen filled with the words unlike anything he'd ever written.

He hadn't been able to type them fast enough, hadn't been able to translate the images of Jesse and Evangeline and their adventure before his mind went on to another scene, and another. Unable to sleep, unable to think straight, he'd started to write even as he told himself that life was over. He needed to leave well enough alone and stop wishing for the impossible.

Still, he'd sat here and typed, amazed that the words flowed so easily, and knew it was because of *her.*

He wanted Alexandra. Desired her. But when she left would the words still come? After being blocked for years and unable to write, was Alexandra the one thing—the only thing—to bring him back? To what end?

Dylan leaned over the desk and quickly minimized the screen, wishing he had the nerve to shut down the computer so that the unsaved document would be lost. A conscious gamble he took because he had nothing to lose or gain.

But a part of him was hopeful and that was the saddest, sickest thing of all. He could yearn for a future all he wanted, but he couldn't change the past or avoid the devastation that would come if he trusted the wrong person or someone discovered his darkest fear.

"You're busy. I'll go."

She turned to leave and he ordered himself to let her. But he couldn't. He moved closer, shifted so that he could slide his hand up and tangle it in her hair.

Her gaze met his, worry and curiosity and wary acceptance in her eyes, as though she knew there was something big between them besides her time limit.

"We're making this too complicated," she whispered, "when it's very, very simple."

A lie. It wasn't simple and he'd bet everything he had that she knew it but was trying to fool herself, the same way he was. Simplicity had gone out the window when they'd agreed to two more weeks. "I don't want you to be sorry you met me."

"Why would I be?"

Such a simple question. He opened his mouth, the truth on his lips. "I've made so many mistakes."

"We all have."

What could he say to make her understand there were mistakes—and then there were *mistakes?*

Alexandra waited expectantly, her expression curious and also sad. "Why are you telling me this?"

"Because you need to know who I was. It took the fire to show me what was important because for a while nothing was as important as *me*. Not my wife, not my son. Nothing."

Alexandra was silent for long seconds and all Dylan could hear was his heart pulsing through his ears.

"So you've warned me," she said softly. "I hear what you're saying but I *still* think you're a good man. And you are so worried about making that mistake that you won't make it again. You're reminded of it every time you look at Colt, and every time you see your hands. Dylan, you're a caring father, a patient son. You work hard and you're aware of your mistakes. It appears to me that the only one who doubts you is you." She tilted her head to the side. "You said she cheated on you. Did you cheat on her? Break your vows?"

It was important to her. Her tone, her expression. And he was proud to stare into Alexandra's eyes and say, "No. Not once."

"Then that's all I need to know. Dylan, I get that your marriage left you with trust issues. It's perfectly understandable. But one day soon? You'll see that I'm not here to hurt you or Colt and you will be thanking God I got on your plane," she said with a teasing smile.

A rough chuckle caught him by surprise. He framed her face in his scarred hands, her words a lifeline whether she knew it or not.

"I already am."

CHAPTER FOURTEEN

ALEX STARED INTO DYLAN'S FACE amazed at how much things could change in such a short period of time. She'd waffled about timing and emotions and fear, but what was she waiting for?

He was a good man, a wounded man, and even though it was wrong of her to think she had the faintest power to help or heal anyone, in this sense she believed she could because Dylan *could* trust her and that was healing in itself.

She had no ulterior motives. No secretive plans. The review was written, her job done, her vacation days, and thus the time she could spend with him, decreasing. What was wrong with holding him, making love with him, easing the wounds someone else inflicted by sharing compassion and warmth? Genuine caring?

She wanted what Dylan was able to give her—himself. She craved his touch and tenderness. Was humbled by the concern for her she saw in his eyes, because he didn't want to hurt her. How many moments in a person's life gave them this much honesty? This wasn't about sex at all. It was so much more. Emotions she was too scared to label.

Alex slowly let the throw drop to the floor. Her hands

found his chest, slid up to the top button of his shirt, then down, undoing them one by one. She'd shut and locked the door on her way into the room, something about the night, his mood and hers, telling her this was it. Everyone was asleep, the house quiet.

When Dylan's shirt was open she pulled his T-shirt from his jeans and slid her hands beneath both, up his rib cage to his tightly muscled pecs. He worked hard and it showed. He wasn't bulky like a gym rat but lean and firm and broad, the perfect size for a woman to lean on. Even the strong independent type like her.

She shoved the material up and was glad when Dylan finished the job, pulling the layered shirts over his head while she tackled his belt and the button of his jeans.

"You're getting ahead of me."

She slid his zipper low, careful of the bulge beneath. "So catch up."

Her husky order set Dylan's hands in motion. He skimmed his palms down her back, over her hips, gripped her behind and lifted her into him until she had to forego her pursuit of getting him naked to balance herself and keep from falling into him in an ungraceful heap. Without a word, without a kiss, he lifted her higher, sliding her up his front using sheer strength, until she wrapped her arms around his neck and her legs around his hips, and bit back a moan when the move brought her thin flannel pants into full contact with the hard length of him.

Dylan somehow managed to swing her around and lower her to the floor atop the throw. And for the first time his mouth brushed hers.

"You're sure?"

Did he believe himself so unlovable? "I'm sure." She might not have a lot of sexual experience but she had enough to discern what was real and what wasn't. This was real. Though flawed and tenuous, it was powerful and true.

Leaning his weight on one arm, Dylan lowered his head for a kiss that used teeth and tongue and unrestrained passion. One kiss, so much feeling.

His lips trailed lower, teasing, nipping the sensitive skin where shoulder and neck met and leaving her awash with goose pimples, clinging to him. His free hand squeezed her breast, his thumb and forefinger tormenting her, before he slid his hand down, lower, beneath the elastic waistband of her pants.

The heat of his breath made her arch, desperate to feel his mouth. Dylan closed his lips over her, material and all. Then off came her flannel pants and underwear and there she lay.

"Beautiful," he whispered against her stomach, kissing and licking until she gasped and felt around for something to hold on to when Dylan gave her the most heart-stopping kiss imaginable.

"Okay?"

She tried to relax but couldn't. No one had ever done that to her. Ever. She'd always considered it too intimate, too…personal. But now?

"Talk to me, sweetheart."

"What do you want me t-to say?"

"Why so tense?"

There was a smile in his voice, one that made her glad she was able to put it there, however unintentionally. "Um…I've never…I mean—" her voice was a bare, revealing whisper "—I have, but not that. I've never had...*that*."

Lying against him the way she was she could feel Dylan's response to her words. His entire body turned to stone, and with the auroras shimmering and rolling outside the window she saw his smile fade. Was her lack of experience a problem for him? A turnoff?

He released a rough sound and lowered his head, pressing a kiss to her belly. "I like the thought of being your first."

She wasn't sure what to do as Dylan shifted lower once more. The tension inside her spread like a fire, her heart pounding out of sync in her chest. All she could do was lie there and feel and hope and wish. Want.

Eyes half-closed, she watched the lights outside the window and tried to breathe when his strokes began again. Slow and soft, teasing. Then harder, firmer. Faster. She arched her back, lifted herself into him. His touch, his mouth, soaring, the sensations too much.

"*Dylan.*" She was on the edge, so close, but she didn't want it to end this way. She wanted to be joined with him, wanted him inside her where she could feel him and hold him because if for some reason this was all they would ever have, she wanted the closeness more than anything else. "Please." She gripped his arms, moved to dislodge him and pull him up her body, but he wouldn't budge. "I want *you.*"

"Shh," he whispered the sound against her, his breath teasing her skin and making her writhe. "I don't have protection in here. It's okay, sweetheart. Let go. For me."

A whimper escaped her at the news. How could she not have considered that fact? Their location?

"I know." He kissed her thigh, nipping it and making her squirm, keeping the tension coiled. "Me, too. But that just means we're gonna have to play until I can get it for us."

Her breath caught in her chest. *Play?* Any more *playing* and she'd be screaming at him to forget it and dive inside, and even drunk with pleasure she knew that wouldn't do.

Dylan smoothed his fingers over her, drawing a moan and a shiver, neither of which she could control.

"Alexandra, let me do this. I want this first. You have no idea how much I want this."

She couldn't say no, didn't *want* to say no. Alex stroked his shoulder, trailed her fingertips down his corded arm and that was all it took.

Dylan kissed her thigh, the jut of her hip bone, and Alex gave herself over to his touch. Every heady caress, every mind-boggling lick took her to that ultimate precipice, held her there for agonizingly sweet moments and sent her flying into the auroras. She gasped, she moaned, she locked her jaw to keep from crying out her release for the house to hear, and through it all Dylan was there, holding her, taking her higher.

Moments later, after her breathing had calmed and she'd released her pleasure-grip on Dylan, he extracted himself and covered her with the throw before grabbing his shirt. "I'll get what we need. Don't move."

She couldn't move if she tried.

Alex heard him shut the door on his way out. And despite the thrill he'd given her, she couldn't wait for him to return. She'd much rather be in a bed, his, hers, it didn't matter, but circumstances being what they were, the loft was the most discreet room in the house.

She rolled onto her side to get more comfortable. He was such a good man. Dylan was solid and sexy and oh, so hot. Gruff but tender. Charming and mannerly. The descriptives could go on forever. He needed to smile more but considering all he'd been through, and was still dealing with, she'd have a hard time smiling, too.

But as the room grew colder and she had to hug her discarded clothes around her for warmth, Alexandra realized something else.

Dylan was a man who went after protection—and never came back.

DYLAN KNEW THE MOMENT Alexandra found him sitting beside Colt on the tiny twin bed. After getting a condom barely in date and splashing his face with ice-cold water in an attempt to get himself under control before he broke the speed record returning upstairs, he'd heard a noise from within Colt's room.

Colt was awake, his eyes glazed in fear, and the tears he'd shed silently in his dreams still wet on his cheeks. Colt shivered and shook and struggled as he tried to push Dylan away, but Dylan held tight the way the docs had instructed, not hurting but not letting go, a solid force that wasn't going to disappear. He was more than willing to fight the demons Colt couldn't, but he was so tired of being shut out, tired of being treated like a stranger.

"What happened?"

At the sound of her voice Colt stirred, listening, but no longer fighting. He was in the present now, not his dreams.

"He had a nightmare." Dylan forced himself to meet her gaze, wondering how she truly felt about Colt's emotional issues. He wouldn't blame Alexandra for thinking them too much. "He'll be fine but I'm going to stay with him until he goes back to sleep. Go on to bed."

Alexandra stared at them for a long moment before she moved into the room. She sat on the edge of the mattress, her fingers stroking Colt's hair away from his face. Without looking at Dylan, she twisted sideways and lay down, Colt between them.

"Mind if I stay, too?"

Apparently that was her answer to his silent question. "Not at all." Alexandra's breast was pressed against his elbow and distracting in the extreme considering what they'd been doing but Dylan couldn't imagine her anywhere else. Her presence was a comfort to him as much as it seemed to be to Colt. He could feel Colt softening, relaxing, as Alexandra lazily trailed her fingertips gently over his eyebrows and forehead.

They lay like that for several minutes, until Colt stopped shaking and the tears slowed. Dylan loosened his hold, knowing the worst was over.

Alexandra raised herself on her elbow and the movement must have startled Colt because in a blink he rolled toward her and threw himself against her, wrapping his little arms around her neck in a tight grip and burying his head in her neck.

"Oh, sweetie. Shh. I'm not leaving, just getting comfortable. See? Let me scooch down. There. Better, yeah? It's okay. You're okay."

Alexandra ran her hands over Colt's back, through his hair, kissed his cheek. And while he watched it all happen, Dylan felt the last of his reservations slipping. He could tell her. He *would* tell her.

"You know, when I was little and I had bad dreams, my mom would come into my room and stay with me until I fell back to sleep, just like your dad," she whispered to Colt. "My mom would tell me stories about when she was a little girl, or we'd talk about what we were doing that weekend or something."

Colt's shoulders lost more of their rigid tension. Even his eyelids were beginning to droop. His son was a heavy sleeper—unless he dreamed. But once he calmed down and fell back to sleep, Colt wouldn't normally awake again until morning. And in the hours between?

"How about I tell you a story? Would you like that?"

Colt rubbed his eyes and moved his head at the same time. A nod? Like the ones Alexandra had described?

A knot formed in his throat. Dear God in heaven, it was. It had to be.

"When I was your age, I lived in a place called Beauty, Tennessee…" Alexandra talked about her home, her horse Bandit, and Thanksgivings and Christmases past and how her entire family gathered together at her parents' mountaintop residence for every holiday. She talked about their traditions like all-day cookie baking and gift wrapping slumber parties.

With every word Alexandra spoke, Colt settled deeper into the bed. Dylan did, too. He liked hearing about the things that were important to her, liked seeing her petting Colt and snuggling him close. Liked that she began to alternately sing and laugh her way through a lullaby completely and totally off-key from the first note to the last and didn't care.

It was an hour before they left Colt's room. Dylan walked the few steps to Alexandra's bedroom door and smiled at the way she couldn't hold back a yawn. "You're exhausted."

"Does he have a lot of nightmares?"

Dylan buried his nose in her hair and inhaled, touched by her concern when she practically wove on her feet with fatigue. "Not as many now."

"I'm glad. His little face broke my heart."

Dylan thought of the moment when it appeared Colt nodded at her and lifted his hand to stroke her hair away from her face. He ran his thumb along the seam of her lips, pausing over the dip in her upper lip. "Pack an overnight bag for your tour tomorrow. If you don't mind spending the night away with me."

Her eyes widened a tad in surprise then sparkled in blatant anticipation. "I'd like that."

CHAPTER FIFTEEN

THE MOMENT THE DOOR OF the Hot Springs Hotel shut behind them, Dylan dropped their luggage and pulled Alexandra into his arms. His mouth found hers and he kissed her, relishing the soft whimper that sounded in her throat when she wrapped her arms around his neck and arched closer.

He framed her face in his palms and ended the kiss, holding her far enough away that he could stare into her gorgeous eyes and search for any signs of misgivings.

"Dylan." Her tone chided, even as her gaze seemed to dare. "Stop thinking so much," she ordered. That said, she pulled him down to her, kissed him again and did that little tongue-swipe thing that made him think of doing the same all over her body.

Maybe they needed this, needed to feel this connection first, then they could move on to the more intense stuff that had to be said.

He took control and kissed her again, his hands sliding to her coat and opening the buttons and belt before he shoved it from her shoulders. He pulled the chamois shirt off, the turtleneck sweater beneath, then set to work on her flannel-lined jeans. He couldn't remove those with her standing so he gently shoved her onto the edge of the bed and gripped her sensible hiking boots. He pulled the strings and tugged the boot off, then he set to work on the other.

Finally all she wore were black panties, a stretchy black tank top over her matching bra, and a single sock that hadn't come off when he'd removed her boots.

Dylan reached for the bottom of the tank top but his hands were firmly moved aside.

"No more until we even things up." Alexandra rose to a kneeling position on the bed and waggled her fingers in a *come here* gesture.

Dylan released the breath he held in a rush and raised his hands in surrender.

ALEX'S HEART RATE SOARED at Dylan's easy acquiescence. He'd had that look again, the one that said he wanted to get serious and *talk*. But she was afraid of what he'd say, afraid of what he'd ask.

Did she want him? Yes, desperately. Did she want more?

That wasn't so easy to answer. So she shoved those questions aside, tilted her head and regarded Dylan. Where to begin?

She pushed his winter coat off his shoulders and set to work on the flannel shirt and thermal beneath. That she pulled from the waistband of his jeans and over his head with a no-nonsense move.

The man was downright *luscious*.

"Like your boots, cowboy. Where'd you get them?"

"They were a gift."

Not being gentle, she yanked at his belt, the snap

of his jeans and when she brushed her fingers against his stomach?

"Alexandra."

"Is there a problem?" His hands settled on her shoulders and slid beneath her hair, and she nuzzled his wrist and palm.

"Don't tease a man in my state, honey." He lowered his head and brushed her mouth with his, his tongue entering her with a seductive stroke that left her toes curled.

When he let her up for air, she ignored the shivers his touch evoked and concentrated on stripping him.

"Jeans won't come off unless you remove my boots."

Dylan lowered himself to the bed beside her with an expression that turned her insides to mush.

"You're going to have to straddle them and pull."

Straddle *him*, he meant. He thought she wouldn't do it? Using every seductive move she'd ever seen in the movies, she shoved him back on the bed and slowly crawled over him, dropping her head to kiss her way down his chest to his navel and earning another harsh inhalation before she got to her feet.

She flashed him a smile and turned to present him with a view of her backside—replete in her best lingerie, picked up at a little shop in Paris.

"You don't play fair."

A laugh bubbled out of her. She couldn't help it. *Play fair?* The man had made her muffle screams and he wanted her to play *fair?*

Grabbing hold of his ankle, she lifted his booted foot and pulled on the expensive footwear. There was a moment of resistance then the boot slid free. One down, one to go. Tossing the leather aside, she slid him another glance over her shoulder and wriggled her rear.

He groaned.

Before she could bend and grab the second boot, Dylan raised his foot even with the bed. The only way to get at it was to swing her leg high.

"You're pretty good at that."

She grabbed the heel, tried not to shiver at the feel of the denim teasing the inside of her thighs, and pulled. This boot took a little more tugging but she got it off and dropped it, then turned to survey her man. Dylan grabbed her hand and pulled her onto the bed on top of him. The moment her knees supported her weight, he sat up, his mouth nibbling at hers.

"We're still dressed," she said between kisses. She ran her hands over his flat stomach, envious of his defined muscles, turned on by the dark furring on his chest and the sensuous trail that led lower. He squeezed her behind, gripped her hips and rocked her against him until she had to lean her head back to breathe. How was it possible to feel like this? To want so much? Care so much?

But not too much.

Dylan shoved the tank top over her head. The front clasp of her bra was nothing to his plucking fingers then his mouth was on her, tormenting her, until she whimpered. "Dylan, don't torture me."

He dropped back, rolled until he was on top and got to his feet long enough to pull a foil packet from his pants before he shucked them and his underwear in one move. He tossed the packet onto the bed beside her and kissed her belly and legs as he tugged her panties off.

From that point their lovemaking turned positively

frantic. Dylan kissed her repeatedly, teased her unmercifully, until she was arching and gasping and clinging to him, moaning his name. Finally Dylan reached for the condom and she did a little teasing of her own while he tried to put it on.

Protection in place, he pinned her down and took her mouth in a possessive, totally alpha way that made her head whirl. Strong though she was, she loved it when a man took charge and Dylan seemed intuitive to her mood.

Moving into position, he gave her body time to adjust, sank a little deeper and stretched her, holding his weight from her until he was fully embedded but kissing her over and over again.

The muted light from the entryway let her see the fierce concentration on his face. And the way he looked at her?

No, that had to be her imagination.

Dylan began to move. Kissing her until she couldn't catch her breath. Doing everything right. He was gentle and rough, sweet and sexy, dominant and totally intent on her pleasure, taking her to climax and muffling her moans of completion before he groaned out his.

When it was over Alex closed her eyes, felt herself sliding deeper and deeper into a well of fear.

Dylan was a good man. A man worth loving for all eternity, not just the limited time she had in Alaska.

But how could she be with him—and still be free?

DYLAN AWOKE WITH A START, his mind unable to assimilate where he was or why he was weighted down. He remembered in a rush and he lifted his hand to cover his eyes, the other tightening ever so slightly on Alexandra's bare hip.

Thankfully, he hadn't startled her and her soft even breaths stirred the hair on his chest. She was draped over him, one arm over his chest, one thigh over both of his.

He tried to find sleep again but seconds later Dylan lifted his lashes and stared at the fire alarm on the ceiling.

Alexandra wasn't heavy by any means but he felt as if he was back inside the dream that had awakened him, unable to breathe, desperate to escape.

He and Alexandra had been dining out in a nice restaurant—a candlelit dinner, soft music, a ring in his pocket. Then someone recognized him and the accusations began. In his dream Alexandra stared at him in horror, every word shouted by those around them making her pale even more. Finally she ran and he followed her, chased her, but couldn't catch her because of the people screaming obscenities, calling him a murderer and getting in the way of his pursuit.

The dream was a reminder of what reality could bring if he told her who he used to be before she left for home.

Dylan kissed Alexandra's forehead, wishing he could rewrite the past, wishing she never had to know and they could go on as they were. That they could be happy.

Alexandra shifted against him, her lashes fluttering. Dylan didn't move, unsure of whether he wanted her to awaken when his thoughts were so dark.

Her hand rubbed over his chest. "You're not asleep." Alexandra nuzzled him and kissed him, right over his heart. "Please don't tell me I've drooled on you—or worse."

"Worse?" He smoothed her silky hair back from her face when she lifted her head. With the entry light turned off, he couldn't make out her features but it didn't matter. He'd memorized them. Black hair, long and sleek, full mouth, cute nose, her gorgeous eyes.

"Saying embarrassing things in my sleep, snoring." She made a sleepy sound and snuggled closer. "So why are you awake? Are you worried about being away from Colt?"

"A little but I know he'll be fine. I've left him with Zeke before, and Walt and Ansel fuss over him like mother hens."

"I used to love spending the night with my grandparents. Still do. Gram is so much fun. We have a blast together."

From the sounds of it, she'd had a happy childhood. So had he.

That's what Colt deserved, too, that same happiness.

He thought of Colt and Alexandra together, coloring, playing, walking outside and throwing rocks into the lake to see who could make the biggest splash. She was good with Colt, patient. Motherly. She'd be a wonderful mother.

Alexandra balanced herself on his chest, her eyes glittering in the darkness. Dylan lost himself to the sensation of her skin next to his and skimmed his fingernails over the silky texture of her hip.

He made love to her again, and this time their pace was slower. He savored every breathless whisper, every moan, aware that time was running out.

THAT EVENING WHILE DYLAN WENT to check on the plane, Alexandra dug out her computer, called the desk for Internet service and sent an e-mail to her boss with the review and photos attached. That done, she checked her account and took care of the few things that needed attending to.

Her cell phone was next. She was so used to not having service that when she turned it on and saw those little bars, she couldn't help but smile. Civilization, gotta love it.

She had numerous missed calls and voice mails waiting for her, along with quite a few texts. Most were from David, all of them harping on the fact she hadn't checked in with him to say she's okay, and to tell her he needed her review ASAP because there had been a problem with one supposed to go in the December issue.

She'd warned him she'd be out of touch but David was as bad as her family. Being her boss only made his concern worse but he had the extra excuse. How could she check in with no signal?

Not in the mood to talk to him, she pulled up one of his texts and typed.

Everything's fine. Enjoying AK. Review sent. Stop worrying.

She sent that and went on to the next message from Luke.

Call home. Mom's freaking out because you've been unavailable so long. PS—Shelby's acting strange again. Yes, I know you two are still at odds after the fight but do me a favor, get over it and call. She says nothing is wrong but she'll tell you the truth.

Luke's message sounded worrisome. What was up with Shelby? Alexandra clicked on the next text. *Bingo*. It was from Shelby.

I'm sorry, okay? I shouldn't have shut Luke out but we're okay now. Where are you in AK? Need to talk.

She'd sent a second one:

How's it going in Man-ville? Find one to keep you warm on those cold Alaskan nights?

Alex rolled her eyes. *Man-ville?* Most people still remembered the old days of the Klondike when the male to female ratio was eight to one but that wasn't the case anymore. It was true that most hunting and fishing lodges were nearly all male, but the male to female population had evened out over the years in the larger cities. As to finding a man to keep her warm... Focusing on the reminder of how well Dylan warmed her up, Alex scrolled down, unprepared for Shelby's next line.

Need to talk. Went back to doc for my checkup after DNC. Everything fine. More than fine. I'm pregnant. Again. And totally freaking out!!! The doc said it has happened like this before. Yes it's fabulous, but what if something goes wrong like last time? Talk me off the ledge. Can't tell Luke yet. Too soon. Don't want him to worry. Yes, we're fine now but new job is keeping him busy. Sorry for being a pain after the accident. Really. Doing better now and wish you were here. I need you, Lex. I'm getting my hopes up.

Smiling and happy and worried all at the same time, Alex said a prayer for a healthy pregnancy and easy delivery, sensing deep down that this time everything would be all right.

Luke and Shelby's loss had nearly destroyed their marriage and Alex didn't want to see that strain happen again. Shelby's response explained the weirdness Luke sensed, though, and Luke really ought to know.

Alex debated whether to bite the roaming charges and call Shelby. She needed to talk but the thing was, her friend could always read her like a book and Shelby would know immediately that something was up. And what would she say? *Man-ville is beautiful and, oh yeah, I just slept with the greatest guy. He's got a kid, takes care of his dad and I'm leaving them in a matter of days so it's just sex—but I love him.*

Her heart stuttered in her chest.

She *loved* him?

Alex sat there, shocked to her core. She couldn't *love* Dylan. Not the long-term, golden anniversary kind of love. It was too fast. Real love didn't happen that way. It was slow and built over time, right?

What she was feeling was infatuation, tenderness. Not love.

Nodding to herself, she hit the reply button, her hands trembling as she wrote:

Man-ville is gorgeous. Taking lots of pics. I'm sorry, too. Glad you two made up. Talk to Luke, he'll be thrilled and he'll understand why you're scared. You need to lean on each other until you're comfortable telling the rest of the fam. Take care of yourself and don't overdo. Breathe. Have faith. It'll be okay.

The door to the room opened with the sound of a sliding key card and the metal-against-metal scrape of the latch. Dylan walked in and her body heated at the sight of him. She hit the button to send the text and tossed the phone aside.

Yeah, Man-ville was great.

So great...she kind of wanted to stay.

CHAPTER SIXTEEN

LATER THAT AFTERNOON, Alex was fresh from the shower and ready to explore. "Come on, come swimming with me in the hot springs."

Dylan flipped down the edge of the newspaper and gave her a regretful shake of his head. "No, thanks. I don't swim much."

Did that mean he didn't like to swim, didn't know how to swim? She found that hard to believe considering he lived on a lake and went fishing all the time. "I'll teach you."

"I know *how,* Alexandra. I don't want to."

"You don't like to swim?"

"I like it fine."

He knew how to, he liked it. What was the problem? Something wasn't right. She crossed her arms over her chest, not about to give up. "Then why not swim?"

Inhaling, he finally said, "I don't like crowds. You go on without me."

She frowned at that. She knew Dylan didn't like crowds—that was obvious given his desire to live in the middle of a wilderness—but they were here and they were alone and swimming together would be fun. It was the only one of her excursions that involved getting in a pool.

Couldn't he compromise? Pretend for an afternoon? It wasn't as though there were *that* many people there.

When she glanced at him and made eye contact, she saw a sad awareness in his eyes. He knew she wanted to go, knew he was disappointing her. So why not meet her halfway? She wasn't asking to go to a stadium full of people for a ball game.

"Go change. Enjoy yourself."

Dylan went back to reading his paper and Alex dug her bathing suit out of her duffel, searching until she found the bright red two-piece with strings and a piece of U-shaped metal that held the material over her chest. Fine, he didn't want to go. But she wasn't going to sit in the room while Dylan read the paper, of all things.

She tossed the bathing suit on the bed and was about to try to find her lotion when she noticed Dylan eyeing her suit from behind his newspaper, a dark frown on his face. Smiling to herself, she had a brainstorm and dropped the towel.

A muffled curse came from behind the paper and it rattled again. Dylan cleared his throat. "How long do you think you'll be?"

She bent and stepped into the suit, slowly pulling the bottoms up her legs. "Not long. But I *can't* come all this way and not get in the pools. That would be such a waste." The elastic settled into place on her hip bone with a *snap*. "I really wish you'd join me. I love the feel of the water on my skin. It's very relaxing. We could find a nice quiet spot and just sit there if you like."

She picked up her top and by the time she put it on and pulled and tucked and straightened and tied, the newspaper was on the floor and Dylan was on the edge of the bed. "Alexandra…"

She looked up, trying her best to look innocent.

Dylan swallowed, the sound rough. "Is that…new for your trip?"

She hid a smile. At least he hadn't gone with the old *You're wearing that?* question that got so many guys into trouble. "You like it?" She did a slow turn, modeling it for him. Like every woman she had a hard time finding a suit that fit right, was comfortable and still somewhat modest. She'd known the moment she'd tried this one on that it was the suit for her. She'd bought three of them, the red one she now wore, a black one and a deep purple one.

"It's…you're beautiful. Maybe I'll…walk down to the pool with you. I'll get dressed and get my coat."

"And sit there in the cold beside the pool instead of in it? No, you can't do that," she said firmly.

"Alexandra, I didn't bring trunks. I didn't plan to swim."

"They have at least three different places selling bathing suits here." She walked over to him and rested her forearms on his shoulders, clasping her fingers behind his head. "Tell you what, I'll run to the gift shop really quick to buy you trunks. We'll go swim, play and later…we'll stay in and do whatever you want."

He pulled her to him, fitting his head directly in the little bit of cleavage she had, his mouth on her skin. Her body immediately heated up from his touch, especially when his hands cupped her behind and his thumbs slid beneath the elastic.

"Whatever I want?"

She smiled, seeing the indecision in his eyes. She

could tell he wanted to go with her but was letting something hold him back. She had to convince him, show him that he could forget his scars and have some fun. "*Anything*. Now, what color do you want?"

His grip on her butt tightened and squeezed. "Blue," he growled like a grumpy bear.

"Thank you," she whispered. "I didn't want to go alone." Alex started to pull away when he tugged her back.

"It's just swimming."

DYLAN SPENT NEARLY THE ENTIRE next week taking Alexandra flightseeing. The places she wanted to see were widespread, so it took hours flying to and from the destinations.

They flew over Mount Redoubt so she could photograph the top and the little puff of steam rising into the air from the active volcano, Mount Spur, she gaped at the blue of the glaciers and she downloaded hundreds of pictures after every trip.

Playing with Colt and listening to Zeke and the men talk was the entertainment of their quiet evenings at the lodge but Alexandra didn't seem to mind, which raised his hopes that she could get used to a simpler life, maybe even like it. That she could get used to living there? Staying there?

Surprisingly, swimming in the hot springs had been fun. Several people were rude enough to stare at his scars, but whenever it happened, Alexandra made a point of reaching out to grasp his hand, cracking a joke or doing something to draw the attention from him to her.

But more important, no one recognized him, and aside from the attention his scars drew, no one seemed to notice him otherwise.

It was a good realization to have after spending so much time alone. Maybe enough time had passed and Zeke was right that Dylan was the only one holding on to the past. Maybe he could do more than dream of a future with Alexandra.

While he carried his sleepy son to bed and tucked Colt in, Alexandra grabbed her pajamas and toiletries to wash her face. Dylan would have liked Alexandra to join them but that was one ritual she said she wouldn't intrude upon. He knew why she kept her distance from Colt and their father-son time but Dylan also hoped if he could get her to agree, she might begin to see herself in their lives rather than passing through.

Minutes later Dylan entered the small bathroom and stood behind her, his broad shoulders dwarfing hers in the little mirror.

Zeke and the others had built another bonfire and if they held true to form, they wouldn't come inside for another hour or more.

Dylan waited and watched while she rinsed her face and patted it dry. He could watch her perform the simple chore for the rest of his life and not get tired of it.

Alexandra lowered the towel she held, her fingers clutched it as if she could read his thoughts. She wanted no pressure and he'd tried to adhere to the rule but with every day that passed it became harder to imagine her gone.

Holding her gaze in the mirror, he saw her eyes darken with a hint of fear. Not of him physically, but, if he had to guess, of what she saw in his eyes when he looked at her.

"Dylan...*don't*."

It was a warning, one daring him not to trespass, daring him not to say the words because she wasn't ready.

He kissed her temple and turned her to face him. The pulse in her throat picked up speed, matched the pounding in his chest. Dylan stared into her eyes and kissed her as he wrapped an arm around her waist, lifted her off her feet, and carried her through the bathroom door to his bedroom.

In seconds they were naked, the tension in the bathroom carrying to the darkness of his bedroom. There wasn't time for foreplay, neither of them seemed to want it. He took care of protection and slid home, muffling the low sound she made with his mouth. Taking her hands in his, he carried them above her head and pinned them there, controlling her movements and bringing her to the very tip of pleasure, all the while watching her, his gaze never faltering, never letting *her* close her eyes or look away.

Her fingers gripped his hands and she arched her back, her gaze heated and revealing as he drove her and himself over the edge.

Dylan left the bed briefly to take care of the condom but immediately returned to spoon her from behind. She fit into his arms perfectly.

He held her, feeling her body begin to relax and twitch with sleep. And because he couldn't keep quiet any longer, couldn't *not* demand more, he pressed his nose into her hair and whispered, "Stay."

"STAY."

· The next day even the roar of the Super Cub's engine couldn't drown out Alex's thoughts. Last night as she'd fallen asleep she could have sworn she'd heard Dylan say the word. But in that place between wakefulness and sleep, had she imagined it? Because she *wanted* to hear it?

She'd crept to her room in the wee hours of the morning to be in her own bed when the lodge awakened. When she saw Dylan at breakfast he'd acted as though nothing had happened, reinforcing her thoughts that her mind had supplied the word, not him.

So was that what she wanted to hear? What she wanted him to say? Demand? What about Colt's issues? What about her job? The review and the fact she'd never told Dylan about it?

Sitting behind Dylan in the two-seater Super Cub, she stared out the window at the vastness of land below, deciding she wasn't sure. A part of her wouldn't mind a few words to let her know what she meant to him besides his obvious physical reaction to her, but knew there had been a couple instances—one of them last night in the bathroom—when she'd warned Dylan not to press and he'd heeded her request. It was her own fault she was so confused because she kept shutting Dylan down when he tried to talk to her. She couldn't demand no pressure from him and not give it herself.

"Look down. That's the land I told you about."

She looked down and saw—nothing. Thinning trees, lots of snow. She didn't see any buildings or people. That was the land? Maybe she'd missed the houses and they'd flown over without her seeing them?

After twenty more minutes the land flattened as they neared their destination. This part of Alaska was the opposite of the area around the lodge. It was wide-open, with no signs of trees.

Finally they flew over the half-dozen homes on the wind-barren plain and circled around for landing. The houses weren't elaborate—simple boxes that nearly blended into the snow-covered ground. Only the smoke coming from chimneys and the people spilling out of one of the doors revealed the life inside.

On the ground, Alex looked around quickly before Dylan introduced her to Owen Foxx and his wife, Kate, their children Marcus, Kyle and the youngest, Sarah.

"What a wonderful surprise!" Kate said in response to Alex's presence.

Once all the niceties were out of the way, Kate led Alex over the snowpack to her home. "Come in and warm up while the men unload the supplies," she said. "Please, make yourself comfortable. Other than the supply drops we rarely have guests, especially women." Kate flashed a bright smile. "And look at you. You're so glamorous."

Alexandra blushed at the description. "Thank you," she said with a laugh as she pulled her hat from her head and went to work on the buttons of her coat.

"Have a seat in the living room while I make us some tea. Or would you prefer coffee?"

"Either is fine. Don't go to any trouble."

"No trouble at all. The others will be in soon."

Alex moved into the living room Kate indicated, taking in the simplicity and the homey feel. "Your house is lovely."

Kate was busy at the stove, so Alex continued looking about, noting their computer setup and plastic containers of school supplies stacked neatly nearby. Turning, her eyes widened when she noticed a wall stacked floor to ceiling with books and magazines. Tilting her head to one side when she spied a familiar spine, she headed toward the stack. "Looks like you get a lot of reading done."

Kate popped her head around the corner and laughed. "It's an addiction. The summers are short and the winters are long."

Alex picked up one of the magazines. *Traveling Single?*

"Have you heard of it? It's a vacation magazine," Kate said from the kitchen. "Owen teases me about the single part saying I'm planning my divorce, but I like it. Those are all old issues Zeke gave me when he was done with them. I get the new ones through an online subscription now but I can't bear to destroy those. I like being able to turn the pages."

"Are you planning a trip?" Alex asked, seeing a mix of romances, mysteries and biographies amongst the shelves.

"I am. I've gone to New Zealand and Australia and to Hawaii, but I'm not sure where I want to go next."

"Does your husband have a preference?"

Kate's laughter drifted into the living room. "Oh, he's not going. Not that I don't want him to," she clarified, "it's just that he never does. Owen got hurt on the job a while back and sitting for long periods of time is painful for him. That's when he began to carve. But, I love to travel and need to get away sometimes, to be someplace warm. We've had our share of arguments over it, but even Owen says I come home a new woman."

Alex tucked her hair behind her ear, Kate's words bouncing around in her head. She could identify with how Kate felt all too easily. Suppose Alex decided to stay, would that be her future with Dylan? Traveling alone, even though she wasn't single? She'd practically had to drag Dylan into the hot springs, and he'd said that day when she'd held the flashlight under the cabin sink for him that he didn't travel.

Opposites were supposed to attract but how well could she and Dylan get along if that was such a personality issue? Seeing him interact with Ansel and Walter and, later, the hunters, Dylan didn't seem like an antisocial guy. He joked, he got along with people. So what was the problem?

Kate and Owen's children burst into the kitchen and the small home was filled with the sound of stomping feet. Their mother waved a hand toward a doorway to the left of the kitchen. "Boys, go play in your room and no interrupting, okay? You know the rules—blood or fire *only*. Keep an eye on Sarah, too, and let me have some girl time with Alexandra. I'll give you each one of those lollipops we've been saving if you behave."

Instead of complaining about having to care for their sister, Alex was surprised when the boys readily agreed and the three took off to their rooms.

Kate pulled out a wooden tray and gathered coffee mugs from a cabinet. "So…you and Dylan. Is it serious?"

CHAPTER SEVENTEEN

TAKEN ABACK BY THE QUESTION, Alex blinked. "Um…"

"Sorry, but we don't have time for skirting an issue when visits never last long," the other woman said with a laugh. "And I need something to focus on besides the kids and me trying to keep up with their schoolwork. Don't be shy. It's obvious you two are together. I saw the way he looked at you out there. Oh, you're blushing. How sweet is that."

Alex put her hand to her cheek. She could feel the heat in her face and it made her feel like a girl with her first crush. But with Dylan she felt that way, all out of sorts and unsure.

"Dylan's a good man, don't you think?"

One of the best. In the two weeks she'd known him she knew she'd never meet another man like him. "Yes, he is."

"So?"

So, Kate wasn't going to drop the line of questioning until Alex answered. Too bad she didn't know the answer. She liked Dylan, she had fun with him. But how serious could it be at this point? Three weeks? Could she really be in love with him? Half of her balked at the thought but the other half… "It's complicated."

"Ah, so it *is* serious," Kate said.

Something in her expression must have given her confusion away. Kate leaned her shoulder against the doorway between the two rooms and studied her with a knowing expression. And because she couldn't pick up the phone and call Shelby to talk out her feelings, Alex knew Kate was her best—and only—female option. "I'm here on vacation," she said simply. "But Dylan and I started talking and connecting. We were supposed to be friends. No pressure, no promises, that's what we agreed to."

"And now that's changed?" Kate asked, her tone soft with understanding.

Why did Alex find it easier to talk to a total stranger than the man making her feel this way? "My life, my *family* is in Tennessee."

"You can build a new life. Isn't life whatever you make it? Wherever and with whomever you make it?"

The door to the small house opened once again. Dylan stepped inside and the sight of him brought a welcoming smile to her lips.

What if that whisper wasn't her imagination? Could her *wherever* be in Alaska? With Dylan and his son?

Feeling Kate's gaze on her, Alex made eye contact and saw the other woman arch her eyebrow, as though Alex's response to Dylan was her answer.

OVER THE NEXT HALF HOUR Alex and Kate talked while Kate prepared a dinner of soup and fresh-baked bread. Dylan listened to the women's conversation, wondering what Alexandra thought of the Foxx's humble abode. Did she think it too plain? Would she like a home like it? One a little fancier?

Owen leaned his chair back on its hind legs, reaching behind him to the buffet and snagging something from the top. "Look at my latest," he said to Dylan. "Think that'll go over well in the shops?"

Dylan picked up the elaborately carved bird, turning it over in his hands. "It's a fine piece of work. Speaking of which, Alexandra wants to see your workshop. She admires Colt's play set and would like to pick up some pieces for her nephews." Dylan went on to explain how she was photographing Alaska.

"I was hoping I could take some pictures, too," Alexandra said to Owen and Kate. "If you don't mind. I'd love to get some photos of you working on your creations. They're absolutely beautiful."

"My ugly mug would break your camera," Owen said with an embarrassment-filled but flattered glance at his wife.

"Tell you what, you let me get you in action as you work, no posing involved, and I'll take some photos of your kids for free and send them to you. Is it a deal?"

Her ploy worked because Kate immediately turned to her husband with a pleading expression, and Dylan was transported back to that day he'd caught Alexandra photographing Colt.

Seeing Kate's face he understood exactly what Alexandra had tried to convey that day. What parent didn't want pictures of their children? Didn't want to capture their child's young years because they grew and changed so fast?

All photos of Colt had been lost in the fire and in the two years since, he hadn't even thought of having Colt's picture taken professionally, not only due to the flight to Anchorage it would entail but also due to Colt's problems. The past two years had been sad years, not happy ones. But since Alexandra's arrival, Colt was smiling more. Playing. Dylan wanted photos to document the strides his son was making. Colt was only this age once.

He'd ask Alexandra to take some shots of Colt. Maybe even of him, Zeke and Colt together since they were three generations and they didn't have any photos of that type. Colt's smiles were infrequent but Alexandra could capture him playing with his wooden horses, tossing rocks into the lake. Being himself.

"I suppose I could stand there and work." Owen's expression softened as the big lug gave in to Kate's look and accepted Alexandra's offer. "The woodshop is out back. I normally wear something like this but I could change."

"Absolutely not," Alex said, taking in the man's coveralls and working clothes with a sweep of her eyes. "You're perfect just as you are."

A surge of something hit Dylan right between the eyes. Jealousy, envy. Sadness. He wanted to be perfect in Alexandra's eyes. Imagine that. Damaged goods like him...perfect.

DURING HER TOUR OF OWEN'S workshop, Alex purchased toy sets for her nephews, as well as a very special horse to add to Colt's collection. Once she was back in Anchorage, she'd ship the play sets home for Christmas.

Alex hugged Kate before she climbed aboard the Cub and took her seat behind Dylan's, sad that the day was over. Would she ever see Kate again? The thought brought another wave of indecision.

She was not only getting totally attached to Dylan, but others here, too. Zeke and Colt, Ansel and Walter, now Kate and Owen. They had fast become her friends.

Maybe even her family?

Dylan was everything she wanted in a man. So was she simply going to walk away when her three weeks were over or was she going to talk to him about how she felt? If he asked her to stay, what would she say? Yes, because she'd like to see how things would develop, where their relationship would go?

Or no, because people didn't do those types of things after such a short amount of time. It would mean giving up everything she held dear, sacrificing so much. Too much?

She and Dylan were both quiet on the flight home, the engine droning and giving them a good excuse to not shout into the headsets at each other to be heard over the noise.

When they flew over Deadwood Mountain Lodge and she looked out the window to see the structure surrounded by nothing but water and trees and mountains, Alex was reminded of the solitary existence Owen and Kate led on the frozen tundra. Kate Foxx had been so happy for company she'd nearly been beside herself, and Alex had felt guilty leaving the lonely young mother because she could feel the other woman's need for more companionship.

She spent a lot of time away working for *Traveling Single* but she returned home to Tennessee every couple weeks to visit. She was a gypsy, true, but she couldn't imagine not being able to see her friends and family whenever she wanted. David was so good about letting her schedule reviews around birthdays and celebrations, holidays.

Staying, *living,* in Alaska would mean not seeing them for very long periods of time. Months, possibly. Would she be able to agree to that?

"Look," Dylan said.

Her gaze fastened on the landscape outside the plane's window and she saw Colt running out into the open to stare up at them. Camera in hand, she watched.

"He's smiling," Dylan shouted. "Take the picture!"

She didn't hesitate. It was quite a concession to have Dylan's permission and she knew it represented the trust he'd placed in her. He was healing.

Alexandra captured their homecoming from the sky. Colt *was* wearing a big, happy, welcoming smile. What a glorious sight, a smile the likes of which only children can give. Her heart felt full, her chest tight.

Maybe she *could* do this. Maybe she and Kate could travel together and see the world. Maybe Dylan would ask her to stay and her family would understand why she'd say yes. Life was about compromise, right?

Dylan landed and when she exited the plane, Colt was waiting for them on the dock, hesitation etched on his little face.

On impulse she dropped to her knees and opened her arms. Colt charged forward, filling the empty space she hadn't even known was there. She held him close, kissed his cheek and sighed.

Maybe….

DYLAN STOPPED CHOPPING WOOD long enough to watch Colt tug Alexandra by the hand to the rear of the lodge.

There was nothing back there but Colt's tree house. Approximately ten feet off the ground, it had a slide and tire swing hanging from a thick limb. Was that where they were headed? It was Colt's place, one he didn't typically share.

Dylan anchored the ax into the chopping block with a sharp *whack* and followed at a distance. Sure enough Colt had led her to the tree house and was already waiting for her to climb up but Alexandra's foot kept slipping on the narrow boards nailed into the tree in ladder-form.

"Sorry, sweetie, my boots are too big or something. I don't think I'll be able to— *Oh!*"

Dylan surprised Alexandra by gripping her slim waist and lifting her off her feet. Once she latched on to the wood, he filled his hands with her fine behind and pushed her the rest of the way, squeezing and copping a feel in the process. Laughing, the sound breathless, she rolled over onto her butt and regarded him from her perch.

"I'll remember that," she promised with a twinkle in her eyes. "Colt, your daddy is ornery, you know that?" She turned to regard Colt, saw the boy's smile and pretended outrage. "*What?* You think that's *funny?*" she asked, leaning sideways to tickle Colt.

His smile grew bigger, wider, and a short sound escaped him.

Dylan froze where he stood. A laugh. Was that a *laugh?*

The sound was gone in an instant. If Alexandra heard it, she didn't let on but when the boy snuggled into her arms and buried his head against her thick coat, Alexandra's gaze met Dylan's and held with meaningful intent. She'd heard it, too. She winked at Dylan, blowing him a kiss over top of Colt's head.

Dylan reached out and caught her booted leg, held it close to his chest because he needed contact with them.

This moment, this peace, this was what he'd waited all his life to feel. Whether she knew it or not, Alexandra held his very heart in her hands.

CHAPTER EIGHTEEN

HER LAST DAYS AT DEADWOOD Mountain passed much too quickly as she and Dylan traveled to the last of her chosen destinations.

When the visibility was too poor to fly and the temperature too cold to travel by boat, she'd pitted her skills against all the men skeet shooting—and won, thanks to a lifetime of target practice with her family. After a lot of ribbing and jokes, she proved that nobody should mess with a Tennessee girl with a gun in her hands.

Yesterday Dylan had taken her and Colt both to tour an old abandoned mining town and showed them how to pan for gold. With every dip of the pan in the water and every smile Dylan gave her, she fell more deeply in love. Despite the cold and the snow, it was a great day, one she didn't want to end. Which is why she'd broken her rule and joined Dylan at bedtime when he went to tuck in his son and listen to the night's story.

As of last night when she'd downloaded and backed up her pictures for safekeeping, she'd noted that during her three weeks in Alaska, she'd taken nearly six thousand photos. Her favorites? Those of Dylan, Colt.

She had been surprised when Dylan had asked her to take photos of Colt but she supposed she shouldn't have been. All it had taken was time for Dylan to trust her. Considering Colt's solemn demeanor, she'd given herself creative license and tried hard to make the photos unique since it was nearly impossible to catch Colt smiling. She strove to capture moments when Colt's expressions revealed his thoughts and concentration. She'd also taken one of Dylan and Colt from behind, where the focus was on Dylan's large, scarred hand holding the small unspoiled hand of his son.

Now it was time for her to return to Anchorage to tour the city. Would Dylan make her go alone? He didn't have the excuse of ill health like Owen Foxx. She'd waited and hoped and prayed for Dylan to say he wanted to come with her. Or even to say that she *needed* to stay because he felt the same way she did and he couldn't imagine life without her. But so far he hadn't.

Now Alex stood in the doorway of Colt's room and watched Dylan's son color a horse in one of his coloring books. Her bags were packed and waiting for her in the hall, and she'd said goodbyes to Ansel and Walter before they'd left for another day of fishing, and Zeke who was in the kitchen cooking lunch.

God, give me strength. I don't know if I can leave without making a fool of myself.

So why leave? Since when had she become a woman who waited for things to happen rather than made them happen? Why not tell Dylan she'd changed her mind, be honest about her freaked-out feelings and see what he said?

What happened to no pressure?

She wouldn't apply pressure. If Dylan didn't feel the same way, so be it. She'd go to Anchorage alone.

And the review?

She'd explain. She couldn't help it if she'd come here to do a job. He'd be upset, but surely he would forgive her?

Outside, she heard the sound of a plane circling the lake to land. Sam had arrived with more guests. The noise of the plane landing caught Colt's attention and he glanced up, spotting her in the doorway. His beautiful brown eyes were sad with awareness. He knew what today was.

Forcing a smile in case she did wind up in Anchorage alone, she moved closer to Colt and knelt on the floor. Not having a sack or bag to wrap the horse she'd purchased for Colt, she'd used a pillowcase. "Hey, it's almost time for your dad to take me to Anchorage. I want you to know how *great* it was to meet you and play with you, Colt. You are a very special, very smart little boy and I will *never* forget you."

Colt dropped the crayon in his hand and rolled onto his bottom, looping his arms around his drawn up knees as he stared at her.

Oh, that look, that sweet little face. She'd miss him so much. "I got you a present to say thank you for showing me around and sharing your tree house and being such a good friend. I hope you like it." She set the pillowcase on the floor beside him. "Go on, look inside."

The boy gave her another sad, heartbreaking glance before he unlocked his arms and reached for the package. He pulled out the horse Owen had rapidly painted to match Bandit's markings.

"Maybe if you're ever in Tennessee, your dad will bring you to my parents' house to meet Bandit in person. Until then…I hope you have fun playing with this one. I had Mr. Foxx make him special, just for you."

Colt scrambled to his feet and threw himself into her arms, nearly knocking her over. Alex closed her eyes and hugged Colt tight, trying to memorize the smell and feel of little boy sturdiness, baby soft hair and the waxy scent of crayons.

Before she could get too sentimental or emotional, Colt shoved himself out of her embrace. He tucked the wooden Bandit under his arm, grabbed the pillowcase and held up his other little hand as though telling her to wait.

Alex didn't know what to make of his behavior, especially when Colt backed away slowly, as though afraid she'd ignore his request, then spun around and ran from the room toward Zeke's.

What on earth?

Then Colt was back. Her gaze fell to the sack and she realized by the weightiness of it he'd placed something inside. Colt approached her with a shy smile on his face, and her heart melted on the spot.

Head down, Colt peeked out from beneath his long thick eyelashes, stopping a few inches away from her where she'd remained kneeling on the floor. He held out the sack for her to take.

"For me?" Dylan's familiar footsteps sounded in the hall outside the door and she knew it was time to go but she wasn't ready yet. Out of the corner of her eye she saw Dylan take position by the door, his broad shoulders filling the opening. "Thank you, Colt."

Colt glanced over at his father but immediately turned back to watch her open his gift.

"I love surprises," she told him as she stuck her hand inside. "What is it? Huh? Oh, a book! Did you bring me a book for my flight?"

In the doorway Dylan swore, straightening to his full height. "Alexandra…"

She flipped the hardcover over to the front, surprised to see the title was by one of her father's favorites. Books were expensive, hardcovers especially, and she felt guilty taking one of Zeke's. "Oh, honey, I like it, but are you sure your grandpa won't mind? This is one of my father's favorite authors."

Colt immediately shoved the thick sheath of bound paper over to point at the author's photo on the back cover flap.

Alex glanced down, doing a double take at the man in the photo.

She blinked, laughed softly, but the image didn't change and her smile faded. *Dylan?*

The slant of his head could only be described as cocky. He was clean-shaven and amazingly handsome, smiling into the camera with masculine assurance. But it was definitely him.

Dylan—her Dylan—was Dylan MacGregor? The *novelist?*

How many books had been bestsellers? How many movies had been made from his work? He wasn't an A-list actor or sports figure but all the same in certain circles he was…famous.

For murdering his wife and her lover.

For a moment the room spun and her grip on the book turned slick with the moisture on her hands. She wasn't one of his readers, having heard from her father how gritty Dylan's books read, but she knew who he was, she remembered. According to her father Dylan wrote with the emotion of Nicholas Sparks, the suspense of John

Grisham, the thrill of Stephen King. Which is why at a fairly young age Dylan had gained the popularity of Louis L'Amour for his fresh-voiced Western set novels, rising to fame—then crashing.

Dear God, who could forget the author who'd supposedly *set fire* to his wife and her lover?

She lifted her gaze off the jacket photo and stared at the boots on his feet, unable to believe the irony. She'd recognized those boots—a brand her father had requested after reading Dylan MacGregor preferred them—but not the man. And when her gaze lifted to meet Dylan's, she saw the truth. All this time... All this time and he hadn't told her?

"Colt, go see Grandpa," Dylan ordered, his voice low. "He's making cookies for you."

Alex was barely aware of Colt's head swiveling back and forth between her and Dylan, a frown pulling his eyebrows low because he knew something was wrong.

Pieces of information continued to fill her mind. Pictures, captions. She remembered newsfeeds and tabloid covers of the author in handcuffs, dark glasses covering his eyes. Photos of a toddler and the fervor generated over Dylan's release because so many were outraged he was going to "get away with it" because his movies and books were popular. But evidence had proven Dylan's innocence until—weren't there rumors of an affair with the nanny?

Dylan said he hadn't cheated.

And she believed him. But why not tell her the truth? *Like you told him the truth?*

Alex hugged Colt to her again and kissed his soft cheek. Swallowing the dryness in her throat, she said,

"Thank you for the present. Now go eat a cookie while they're warm." She forced herself to meet Colt's gaze and smile even though it took everything inside her to muster the effort to appear okay when nothing was and never would be again. "That's when cookies are the best."

With one last look, Colt ran out the door. Alex watched him go, the book in her hand as she stood on shaking legs.

"I was going to tell you. Not in the beginning, but when we began to get close."

"But you didn't." And she couldn't even be mad about that because hadn't she done the same?

"I didn't want my past to scare you, to scare you *away.* I wanted you to know *me,* not what others made me out to be."

She knew him. In a way she felt she saw Dylan more clearly than he saw himself. He hadn't told her so as not to scare her but it did. It *did.* Not because she believed he'd had anything at all to do with Lauren's death but because she'd come to Deadwood Mountain Lodge under the guise of a vacationing photographer and *she* hadn't told Dylan the truth of why she was there. How *sad* was that? Neither one of them had been open and truthful. They'd both been deceptive.

She knew how upset Dylan would be that her review would promote the lodge and bring in outsiders, and even now she couldn't force herself to open her mouth and say the words because she knew it would be one more wedge between them when they already had a mountain. "Believe it or not, I understand. Your past is…huge. You needed more time to tell me the truth."

He nodded slowly, his confusion at her easy acceptance evident. "I had to be sure of you, of your reaction and dealings with Colt. You didn't know me well enough to set aside the hype, and I knew if you remembered what happened—which you obviously do—you might not have believed me."

And that was important to him. He hadn't hurt his wife. Regardless of the evidence, she now knew Dylan well enough to not doubt that. "I believe you. I've always believed you."

Relief transformed his face into a smile. "I'm sorry you had to find out this way but I'm glad it's done. Now you know. Alexandra, I don't want you to leave. I want you to stay with me and Colt. I called my attorney when we were at the hot springs. He's made an offer on that tract of land I told you about. We'll leave Zeke to his entertaining and guests and we'll build there. We can have our own life."

She blinked at him, shaking her head slowly back and forth. That track of land flashing through her head. Build there? Stay with him *there?*

After wanting Dylan to tell her how he felt, now that he was she couldn't rid herself of the image of Kate Foxx's stack of books, of her little house on the frozen tundra where she had only Old Maude for company.

Kate had Old Maude but Alexandra would have no one because there was no one there. That wasn't what she wanted. That wasn't what she wanted at all. "I can't. *No,*" she said when he stepped forward as though to take her in his arms.

She didn't want him to touch her. If he touched her, she might try to lie to herself again and for both their sakes someone had to say enough. Someone had to be real. What was she thinking? She'd known him three weeks and suddenly she was going to give up everything to live in the middle of nowhere? Who *did* that? "Stop. I do believe you, Dylan, but this—this is *crazy*. It's only been three weeks and we've been kidding ourselves the entire time."

"What do you mean?"

Him. Her. How could it be so difficult to talk about something as elemental as their *identity?* How indicative was it of their true feelings if they were *both* afraid of the truth?

Three weeks wasn't enough time for someone to choose the right paint colors for a bathroom, much less plan a future with a man she barely knew. She believed him, but was this what she wanted?

Somewhere along the line she'd gotten caught up in the moment. In the passion and fun and sweetness and tenderness, in the adventure of Alaska and Dylan and the romance of falling in love.

But more important, somewhere along the line she'd forgotten it was *just* a fling. "Neither one of us has been entirely honest, that's what I mean."

This was why she didn't get involved. This was why her jet-setting, country-hopping lifestyle suited her so well. A few days here, a week there. Short periods of time that left no chance to get involved, that didn't leave her feeling the way she did right now.

"I don't understand. What have you not been honest about?" A dark look transformed his features. "Is there someone else? Someone waiting for you at home?"

She shook her head, hurting because this shouldn't be this hard.

Dylan moved forward and he didn't stop until he stood directly in front of her, his scarred hands extended but not touching her.

"What is it? Alexandra—"

"No. No, I can't *do* this. We've had a great time but I'm not the person you want me to be."

"What does that mean?"

"I can't live in the middle of nowhere!" she said, blurting out her thoughts and hating herself for it. "And what about *Colt?*" Alex stared at him, her fingers hurting where they gripped the book. Dylan's past, their future. They didn't *have* a future. Not here. Even if he forgave her for her part in the review, what then? Compromise was one thing but total surrender wasn't in her genes.

Her heart pounded in her chest, fighting the hurt of it splitting in two. "Dylan, Colt barely sees people now, and you want to take him farther away?"

"I want to be free to breathe. I want to be away from Zeke's guests crawling all over the place."

"You want to *hide*. Even at maximum capacity the lodge and cabins would hold what? Twenty people?"

"You don't understand because you didn't live it. I don't want to risk going back to that. I *am* thinking of Colt."

"No. No, Colt's fine. He's getting better every day but you've been hiding ever since the fire and I don't blame you. But it has to stop, for both your sakes. Dylan, how far will it take for you to feel safe? How far before you realize you can't run from what happened? If I didn't know you as well as I do, I'd probably believe you were guilty because of how you're hiding away here instead of living your life."

Dylan stared at her, anger hardening the muscles of his face, his eyes that of a man broken. "I'm talking about building a life with you and my son. There's nothing wrong with not wanting to be surrounded by people."

"You don't have to be surrounded. But you do have to be able to *deal* with people and you can't." How sad was it that he couldn't see the difference? That she hadn't seen the difference until moments ago? "That's not building a life, Dylan. That's creating a bubble. You're innocent of Lauren's death but you've let everything you've been through make you afraid. You've trapped yourself here and because people are encroaching, you want to go deeper, to get farther away. You keep retreating, hoping to find a place where no one can trespass and no one can hurt you again. That's not possible."

He wanted her. She saw it on his face, in the way he looked at her. He wanted her as much and as desperately as she wanted him. But for her it was love and for him it was fear—he was afraid yet he didn't want to be alone.

What would he do when he found out about the review and discovered she was the one helping to bring more people to his hiding place, what then?

She knew the answer. He'd be furious. But it didn't matter because right now there were way more important issues to be faced. "I love you," she whispered softly. "If someone had said it was possible to fall in love in three weeks, I would have called them crazy. I love you," she repeated, "but I can't save you, and, Dylan, you *have* to face this because no one can but you. Not Zeke, not Colt and certainly not me. I'm not Kate Foxx," she said, careful to keep her voice low. "I would feel trapped in a place where it's a two-hour *plane ride* to get *any*where."

"People live it every day."

"And it works for them but it wouldn't work for me."
It was getting harder to get the words out. Dylan said
he wanted a place to breathe but she couldn't breathe,
not *here*. Not like this. "Maybe if we'd met somewhere
else. Maybe if you weren't so determined to hide…. My
family would not understand and even though they drive
me nuts on a good day, I wouldn't want to be so far away
I could only see them once a year. And when I did go
home," she said, even though she could see that her
words hurt him, "or I went on vacation, I wouldn't want
to go *alone* and you wouldn't go, would you?"

His eyes blazing with anger and hurt and numerous
other emotions, Dylan shook his head.

Pain stabbed deep in her heart. That wasn't the
answer she wanted. "I love you, I want to be with you,
but not here. Dylan, I *refuse* to give up everything in my
life because you're afraid of yours."

Dylan scowled at her with the look of someone lost
in a sea when he couldn't swim.

Dylan had to save himself. She only hoped he
managed to do it before he dragged Colt down with him.
"Always remember I didn't come here to hurt you…."

Alex dropped the book on the bed as she passed and
thanked God the hallway was empty when she collected
her luggage. Somehow she put one foot in front of the
other. Sam was here. If she could get to Sam before he
took off, he could take her with him. Fly her away. She
didn't care where, so long as it wasn't here.

Her vacation fling was officially over.

CHAPTER NINETEEN

SHE WAS GOING TO DIE.

Alex stared up at the fasten seat belt sign as the jetliner abruptly dipped and rattled through another wave of turbulence. She gripped the armrests and began to pray, her voice drowned out by the shrieks of the three hundred fifty passengers filling the plane.

It's a Wonderful Life droned on from the tiny screen built into the seat in front of her, the earphones useless against the worried chatter and tears expressed by her fellow seatmates. Couples held hands and snuggled close, children clung to mothers and fathers and cried. Alex sat surrounded by people yet totally alone, her gaze focused on the movie, on the child cradled in the hero and heroine's arms.

The plane took another plunging dip as though the very air had been removed from beneath the wings. People screamed as the structure rocked from the force of the wind and rain, and the person in front of her disobeyed the pilot's request and raised their window slide to see how bad it was outside.

Abandoning the happy couple on the screen, she looked outside the window as jagged lightning shot straight for the wing.

Alex awoke with a gasp and bolted upright in her bed. It was only a dream, albeit one she'd lived just hours ago.

She put her hand over her chest and held tight as though that alone might slow her heart's pace. The curtains covered the windows and the hotel room's darkness reminded her too much of that glance outside the plane window.

She rolled to her side and turned on the bedside lamp before dropping onto her pillow and smoothing the hair off her sweaty forehead.

Her flight to Mexico had started off great with a bump up to first class and free drinks. By the time the wheels had touched down she'd struggled to stand on her wobbly legs like everyone else emerging pale-faced from the nightmare in air.

During that flight she'd come to the conclusion that size didn't really matter in anything. It wasn't the size of the plane that mattered. Large or small, the experience could be smooth sailing or a disaster.

No, it was the richness of life and how well it was lived, the people in your life and the dreams that filled it. The love you gave and hopefully received. Those things mattered.

And it was during that plane ride through hell on her way to someone's idea of paradise that she realized she lacked those very things.

She'd come to the hotel and literally collapsed into bed, falling asleep almost instantly from the physical and emotional toll of the experience. Now she was wide-awake and fear uncurled in her stomach as she recognized the truth and intensity of those feelings she'd had on the plane.

It was like that instant oh-my-God-jolt one got when she almost stepped off a curb in front of a speeding bus. Or that knot in the stomach that grew bigger because there was a chance the plane *could* very well go down.

That feeling no one wanted to feel.

It was the sense of momentous regret.

As the family on the airplane's movie screen had smiled their joy and talked of angels and wings, she'd felt that regret all the way to her soul and wondered if she would get the chance to fix it.

If Dylan knew where she was. If he broke out of his shell and came to her...

Like that's going to happen.

It was the truth. Dylan was wrapped up in the world he'd created. He wasn't leaving.

She was alone. But, God's honest truth, she didn't want to *be* alone.

The awareness settled deep and let her identify the thing that had been bothering her for the past year. She hadn't been able to put her finger on what it was but now she knew.

The thrill was gone.

Like the shininess of silver, the thrill had tarnished to a lackluster patina. She used to feel so worldly. But the bedside lamp showed her the truth she'd been avoiding by hopping a plane and going somewhere else every time she began to notice what was absent in her life.

Though nicer than some, this room looked like all the others. A little dingy and worse for wear, more than a bit tired and worn. No matter the simplicity or glitz or style, every hotel room held the same cold bed, the same ugly curtains. The same overwhelming loneliness.

Hotel rooms were meant to be shared. That's why there were either two beds or a king. And the people who should be here with her would have provided the missing sparkle and beauty and shine. They were the life, the joy of the room, not the room itself.

Where was her life? Where was she running *to?*

Where Dylan lived in the prison of his past, where he hid from the world unable to dig himself out, she realized that, for quite a while now, she'd carried her prison *with* her.

She'd used her job as an excuse to avoid her family, to avoid witnessing what they had that she didn't. She'd used it to run, to not get close to a man, to not care too much, not *love* too much because she didn't want to give up the control she'd finally found from being on her own. She enjoyed that freedom.

But she wanted more. She wanted to love and she wanted to *be* loved. And that meant making the conscious choice to slow down long enough for it to happen. It meant not compromising but not avoiding happiness.

She loved Dylan. She wanted to be with Dylan, spend her life with him, but she was also smart enough to know she wasn't strong enough to break him out of his prison and her words to him in Alaska were right on the mark.

He had to stop hiding, she had to start living.

So what now? Where did she go from here?

She mulled that over, staring at the ceiling. Maybe, since her journey with Dylan had begun with a reservation, her future also needed to start with one.

Make sure this is what you want. Make very, very sure.

Once more her heart pounded fast. Alex ignored the frantic pace and leaned over to pick up the phone, punching one of the marked buttons at the bottom with her finger before tossing her blankets aside and moving to the edge of the bed.

"Front desk. Good afternoon, Ms. Tulane, may I help you?"

She closed her eyes and inhaled. "Yes. I'd like to cancel my reservation and book a flight."

FIVE DAYS BEFORE CHRISTMAS Dylan shook Owen's hand and tried not to think about the last time he'd been here and who'd accompanied him.

"Too soon for another supply drop. Did my Christmas orders finally make it?" Owen asked.

"Yesterday. Cutting it close this year. Kate's probably worried, eh?" He and Owen began to unload the plane and by the absence of Owen's kids, Dylan guessed Kate was keeping them occupied inside.

"No, she did most of the shopping for them earlier in the year. Already got it wrapped up and everything. This is for her." Owen gave Dylan a proud grin. "I got her a new set of luggage. She's going to love it."

Dylan grabbed one of the two large shipping boxes and began to follow Owen toward the house, shaking his head at Owen's thinking and remembering Alexandra's last words to him about traveling alone.

And there he went, thinking about her again.

"Better prepare yourself. Kate's going to be disappointed when she sees you and doesn't see your woman with you."

Dylan swore silently. He didn't need Kate's disappointment to deal with when he was already weighed down by Zeke, Ansel and Walter's. Plus his own. And

Colt's. None of them had been the same since Alexandra had walked out the door that day.

They took the boxes directly to Owen's workshop for safekeeping, then Owen led the way into the house for coffee before Dylan's flight back to Deadwood.

In the house the rich smell of pumpkin pie and gingerbread greeted them as they walked in the door. The kids were huddled around the kitchen table hard at work decorating a mound of cookies, but Kate was in the living room working on their Christmas tree, Christmas carols blaring out of the computer speakers. She smiled at the sight of him but, as Owen had predicted, her smile seemed to wobble when she realized he was alone.

"Keep working, Katie. I'll get the coffee. Dylan, have a seat. Hon, you want some?"

"No, thank you." Katie continued to stare at Dylan.

Pressed for something to say Dylan murmured, "That's a pretty tree, Kate."

"It is, isn't it?" She lifted something from a box. "Since you're here, would you mind putting the star on the top? You're tall enough without having to drag out the ladder." She lowered her voice. "And if Owen drags it out, he'll insist on climbing it instead of letting me or you do it."

"I heard that," Owen said from the other room.

"Meant you to," Kate called back sweetly, even as she winced at Dylan.

One slip off that ladder and Owen would be laid up all winter. "Glad to help. Where is it?"

"On the computer table."

He welcomed the reminder. "I've been wanting to ask about your setup for school. Zeke's getting satellite

Internet and I need to get organized for Colt to begin homeschooling." Dylan moved toward the computer and picked up the intricately woven star. He dreaded the complications of trying to teach Colt given his silence but they couldn't stall forever. He glanced at the computer screen and stilled. "What the hell?"

"Oh, don't tell me it's broken," Kate said, quickly rounding the tree. "I just pulled it out and set it aside. I didn't look it over."

Kate took the star from his hand but Dylan didn't so much as blink. He couldn't. All he could do was stare at the computer monitor and the photos of Deadwood and the lake, the cinnamon-colored bear fishing and the pinkish-purple of the northern lights. The pictures could have been taken by anyone but he'd seen those before. He'd been there *while* they were being taken.

"I can't believe you or Zeke didn't tell me a reviewer from *Traveling Single* was at the lodge," Kate said. "I would've *loved* to have talked to him."

"We didn't know," he murmured, anger barreling through him. They hadn't known because Alexandra hadn't said a word.

"It's a great piece. A three point five isn't bad, and since Zeke is upgrading to satellite Internet, they'll probably insert an updated block in a future issue and raise the rating. Zeke must be thrilled. It's great timing, too. You guys will probably have a busy spring with that for advertising."

Alexandra had known how he felt about more guests. But obviously that didn't matter to her, just like telling him the truth of who she was hadn't mattered. He'd felt bad about his identity when all along she'd been keeping a secret, too.

And now that she knew the truth about him?

His gut twisted up like a pretzel. Was a review *all* Alexandra had written?

"The star can wait," Kate said, setting it on the table. "Go ahead and read it while I check on the kids and help Owen with the coffee."

Dylan pounced on the chance and was barely aware of Kate leaving. The reviewer's byline was listed as M. Alex. He didn't know what twist of her name it was but he didn't care. He speed-read the article, looking for anything about him or Colt, searching through the many pictures that had been included in the review.

Alexandra had been shocked by his identity—understandable in itself—but with every one of her adventures at the lodge, she'd been pulling the wool over their eyes.

There wasn't any mention of him or Colt specifically but with every word and every photo his anger grew.

Dylan had to get out of here, had to get away before he yanked the computer off the desk and threw it to relieve the fury inside him.

Alexandra had accused him of hiding. *Hiding* when she was doing the same damn thing. How was he supposed to respond to that?

Dylan knocked the star from the desk when he straightened. It fell to the floor but thankfully didn't damage. He snatched it up, thought of Owen and his damn back and Kate traveling by herself and Alexandra leaving, and jammed it into place atop the tree before he headed for the door.

Dylan heard Kate and Owen calling his name as he

walked out into the cold. He'd have some explaining to do later, but he couldn't do it now.

Maybe Lauren's behavior had slowly eaten away at him until he'd felt nothing but responsibility for her because of the vows he'd made. Whatever the reason, Lauren's betrayal hadn't hurt this much. Neither had Belinda's backstabbing sellout.

Dylan powered up the plane, ignoring the nagging in his head that he hadn't been up-front with Alexandra, so he'd gotten what he deserved.

He was in the air in a matter of minutes and keeping himself there forced him to concentrate on the readings and instruments instead of her. As the forest became thicker and he left the tundra behind, he passed over the tract of land that was for sale, eyeing it from the plane.

Zeke had said he'd known when it was time and he'd needed a new start. Well, Dylan needed one now.

Alexandra had written something that would draw more people to Zeke's lodge and regardless of what she'd said, he didn't consider guaranteeing Colt's safety and future the same thing as hiding. And that land down there—that was their new beginning.

As Dylan flew closer to Deadwood Mountain the radio crackled with a burst and he winced from the pain in his ears.

"Dylan, you there?"

He recognized Zeke's voice in an instant. Surely Owen hadn't radioed Zeke? But even if Owen had, Zeke would've gone through the formalities of radio communication unless…

"I'm here," he stated simply. Was Zeke having another heart attack? "What's wrong?"

There was a second's pause on the other end. "I don't wanna worry you but I can't find Colt. I've looked everywhere for him but I can't find him," he repeated. "You need to get back here soon as you can."

Dylan relaxed a bit. His son had made a habit of climbing into closets or into places small and dark whenever he was bored playing with his horses and toys. "He's there somewhere. Keep looking. I'll bet he's fallen asleep and can't hear you."

Since Alexandra's departure Colt hadn't been sleeping well at night and was often tired during the day. "I'm almost home. Check under the beds and in the loft and keep me posted."

Dylan brought the Cub in for landing, figuring by now Zeke was in the house giving Colt a lecture. The moment he climbed out of the plane, he heard his father's shout.

"Did you see him?" Zeke ran toward him.

"Slow down, dammit. Did you run all the way here?" And then his question sank in. "You haven't found him?"

Zeke slowed to a stop and bent at the waist, his hands on his knees as he drew in ragged breaths. "No. Dylan, I've turned the house upside down. I've looked everywhere. The beds, the closets, his tree house. I can't find him."

Dylan scanned the area for any sign of Colt's dark head, not allowing himself to panic. Yet. "He's got to be here somewhere."

Cold fear was beginning to pour through Dylan's veins. If Zeke had searched all those places for Colt and couldn't find him, the boy didn't *want* to be found. Or he was hurt. Or lost. Where was he?

Not wanting Zeke to overdo it after his race to the

landing strip Dylan said, "Walk back to the lodge and look again. The pantry room and the bathtubs... maybe he's playing a game. I'll take a look around the dock."

Once Zeke was inside the lodge, Dylan ran as fast as he could, calling Colt's name. On the other side of the lake a bull moose lifted his head and hunkered down, ready to charge despite the distance. Was Colt out there? What if he came upon one of the animals and it thought Colt was prey? Attacked? "Colt!"

Every shout brought memories of the fire, the total terror of the unknown, of what he might find when he finally located his son. *"Colt!"*

The dock was clear, the boat empty. The Beaver, too. He ran along the length of the dock far enough to jump to shore, heading toward the storage shed. It was locked up tight. Surely Colt wouldn't have gone to the cabins?

Dylan scanned the surface of the lake, searching for anything, hoping, praying to see Colt throwing rocks into the water, oblivious to the chaos he'd created.

Where was his son? His every breath the past two years had been taken with Colt in mind. He'd worried about Colt, cared for Colt, protected Colt because Dylan hadn't been the father he should've been the first few years of Colt's life. But this was a fist to the gut. It proved he couldn't protect Colt. No parent could.

Had he taught Colt what he needed to know to survive...outside of what Alexandra had coined the *bubble?*

"Colt, *answer me!*" Alexandra's words echoed in his head.

The air left his chest in ragged jags because no matter

where he searched, he saw no sign of his son. "Colt, make some noise so Daddy knows you're okay!"

Nothing. Dear God above, there was *nothing* but the sound of his own voice echoing off the lake and trees.

"Dylan!"

Zeke's shout stopped his heart even as it spurred Dylan to action. He ran up the sloping hill to the lodge, expecting to see Colt standing beside Zeke but only found his father waiting on the porch, his face lined with worry and pale with strain. "Did you find him?"

Zeke nodded repeatedly. "I found him. He's okay— but he's not here."

and scrapbook have accumulated. The envelope had included copies of the photos the student's teacher and I had sent with a message and explanation. The actual files ... stuff was sitting through copies and text. But he wouldn't want a picture of his horse.

... is not her choice.

... ahead. Gotten the photo and knowing that here ... wouldn't ...-serviced the ...-... ...-... ... here ... apprehensive ... got as ... ...

CHAPTER TWENTY

IT TOOK AN HOUR AND FORTY-FIVE minutes for Dylan to refuel and fly to Anchorage. Zeke stayed behind, putting the lodge back to rights after the frantic search and supposedly taking it easy.

When Dylan landed, Ansel and Sam met him at the door.

"Dylan, I'm sorry." Sam glanced over his shoulder to where Walter sat with Colt on the seats in the waiting area. "I had no idea he was on board. He must have snuck on while I was getting coffee."

"He's fine, though," Ansel added, patting Dylan roughly on the shoulder. "No worse for wear at all. Unlike you right now. That was a long flight, eh?"

The longest. Because all he could think about was the reason *why* Colt had snuck onboard Sam's plane. He was running away. "Has he said anything?"

Ansel's face softened. Being frequent guests and friends of Zeke's for a while, they knew of Colt's problem.

"No, son. Not a word. He just followed orders, sat where he was told and has been holding that horse and the photo the whole time."

And they all knew why. Two days ago a packet from Alexandra had arrived in the mail and ever since Colt had been even more withdrawn. The envelope had included copies of the photos she'd taken of him, Zeke and Colt along with a memory stick containing the digital files and a note stating all other copies had been destroyed. Also included was a picture of her horse, Bandit—just for Colt.

Thinking of the review, the photos and knowledge she had access to and the way she could have used them, Dylan lost some of his anger.

"Zeke's guests are getting tired of the delay but I wanted to apologize in person," Sam told him. "I'll be sure to double-check from now on."

From now on? This wasn't going to happen again.

"Had to be scary back there wedged between the bags the way he was." Sam chuckled. "Reminds me of when I snuck on my uncle's plane to hitch a ride into Anchorage for a night on the town. I was ten and bound and determined I was going to get out of no-man's-land and have some fun. I hated being stuck in the middle of nowhere. It's why I soloed at fourteen."

Ten. Fourteen. That was only a few years older than Colt now. And if Colt was sneaking on planes at five, what was he going to attempt at ten and fourteen?

Dylan murmured his thanks for their help and headed for Colt. His son looked up, his eyes widening when he saw Dylan approach.

"See? There he is. Told you it wouldn't be long now, didn't I?" Walter patted Colt's knee and stood. "Dylan, glad you made it safe."

"Thanks." He waited until Walter walked away before squatting in front of Colt. His son was smudged from what appeared to be chocolate but otherwise looked fine as Ansel had said. He wanted to ask *What the hell?* but tempered it with "Were you scared?" He didn't wait for a nod. "Grandpa and I were *very* scared when we realized you were gone. We searched all over for you and when we couldn't find you—" his voice roughened with his fear-fueled anger "—we thought you'd gotten lost or *hurt.*"

Colt dropped his gaze until his lashes nearly dusted his cheeks and two big tears rolled silently down his face.

He wanted to pick Colt up and shake him, do *something* to get Colt to realize the danger of what he'd done, what could have happened to him. Instead he forced himself to take a deep breath and unearthed patience from a source he didn't know he had. "You miss Alexandra, don't you?"

Colt's hands clenched over the horse's flanks. With his head lowered, one of Colt's tears splattered on the picture of Bandit.

Colt lifted his elbow, wiped his face on his coat sleeve.

"Yeah, I thought as much. But no matter how much you miss her, you can't take off like that. Do you understand me? *Never again.* Your grandpa was worried sick and Ansel and Walter have missed their flight home because they stayed here to be with you until I could fly in to get you." His son's shoulders slumped with the weight Dylan applied but he hardened his heart at the sight. Colt had to be made to understand. "Colt, she's *gone.* Alexandra's not coming back, but you're old enough and smart enough to know she wouldn't want you running away like you did." At the end of his rope, Dylan swore silently and stood. "Come on, we have to get back to the lodge and give Grandpa a hand."

Colt didn't move.

"Colt, I said let's go. We need to get in the air before it's too late and we have to spend the night here." When Colt still didn't budge, Dylan lifted his hand to place it on Colt's shoulder only to watch in stunned amazement when Colt ducked to avoid his touch and scrambled out of the seat.

After everything he'd done, Colt did not just— Dylan grabbed him before Colt took more than a couple steps away. Colt immediately began striking out the way he did in the midst of one of his dreams, and despite wanting to turn him over his knee, Dylan pulled his son to his chest, horses and all.

"Noooooo! Alllllex!"

Screamed directly into Dylan's ear, it took a second for the pain to subside and the words to sink in.

Colt had talked. *Yelled?*

Dylan released Colt to hold him at arm's length, staring into Colt's anger-reddened, tear-streaked face.

All this time Dylan had prayed for a laugh but a yell served as well. The relief and happiness he felt at the breakthrough was quickly overtaken by resentment and awareness. Colt's last words were of his mother, and his first after two hellishly long years were for *Alexandra?*

He stared at Colt and fought the pain slicing through him. Was he still such a lousy father?

Thinking about Alexandra's stay with them, Dylan couldn't count the number of times Colt had responded to Alexandra rather than him. The night she'd curled up in bed and sang the lullaby, when they'd played together in the tree house. Now this. Colt didn't respond to Dylan but to her. Always her. And the truth of it stabbed him in the soul. She'd left them and yet he and Colt were still hurting. "She's gone, Colt. Alexandra went home. Now, come on, we're leaving."

Sheer stubbornness crossed Colt's face and he dug in his heels, refusing to budge when Dylan straightened and tugged on his arm.

"Going to see *Alex*." Colt held the horse and photo tighter against his chest.

A rough huff of amazement escaped Dylan. He didn't know whether to laugh or cry. All the worry, the sleepless nights. Colt had been listening, learning, exactly the way the doctors had said he was. And now that Colt had made up his mind to see Alexandra…

"Isn't that something," Walter said, a smile in his voice. "Won't be long before he'll be talking your ear off."

Because Colt was no longer afraid. He was determined, he was fearless. He was on a mission.

The only thing now standing in Colt's way was his own father.

And his father's fear.

Dylan realized he was staring at a little man possessing more guts than he had himself. Colt wanted Alexandra so he was going after her. Period.

Dammit all to hell, his *five-year-old* had the balls to face what he couldn't—the world.

A wave of awareness washed over him and suddenly Dylan knew he was angry at the wrong people. He'd been angry with Alexandra, angry with the world for accusing him when he'd been proven innocent, but more than anything he was angry at himself. He should have fought harder, held his head higher. He shouldn't have run away. Should have stood his ground the way Alexandra had stood hers. She didn't want to be away from her close-knit family, didn't want to live in a bubble.

At least Colt was running *to* something, to some-*one*. He wasn't running away at all. "You want to see Alexandra?"

Colt nodded without hesitation. "And Bandit," he added softly.

And Bandit, Dylan repeated in his mind. Colt wanted to go and do and see, just as Alexandra had said she liked to do on her vacations. She was a travel reviewer used to seeing the world, and even though he hadn't known that at the time, what right did he have to expect her to give up everything because he was—the admission wasn't an easy one to make, even to himself—*afraid* of the past?

He couldn't. He wanted her but if he hoped to keep Alexandra in his life, *he* had to be the one to change. The one to grow. Alexandra was a woman who knew what she wanted and refused to sacrifice it. How could he not respect that?

Who better to help him face the future than the woman he loved? Than the one brave enough to set him straight and walk away, even as she'd said she loved him—and he believed it.

Two hours ago his biggest fear was not finding Colt safe. Now it was staying so rigid he drove Colt away the way he'd driven Alexandra away. Of finding himself on that tract of land, safe, but last man there, bereft in the world he'd made. Alone.

Alexandra had called him on his fears, much as he'd hated her for saying it. Every parent wanted to protect their child, but how long would it be until Colt hated

him? Resented and rebelled? Colt's five short years had
passed in a blink of an eye and it wouldn't be long
before he was old enough to decide whether to stay or
go on his own. And looking at the boy in front of him
Dylan knew what Colt's answer would be.

Colt squirmed in Dylan's hold.

"Can we go see Alex?"

Could they? Even if he tracked her down and
managed to make amends, what about her family? How
would they react to the news of who he was? What he'd
allegedly done?

You going to let fear stop you? Again?

No. Because she was the one. She was the one who
made him want more, to dream of everything, a future.
The one who unblocked his muse, who made him smile
and remember how to love. She held his heart in her
hands because she was the one who'd opened his eyes
and made him realize he *was* holding Colt back and he
was going to lose *everything* if he didn't wise up.

It may have taken him a while to get his head on
straight but now that he had, he wouldn't make the same
mistake twice.

ALEX STARED AT THE PATHETIC-looking, spindly tree and
knew it was perfect. With its drooping branches, minia-
ture stature and total lack of fluffy big tree appeal, it
suited her mood perfectly.

"You cannot be serious."

Shelby made the statement as she walked up to stand
behind Alex where she stared at the wannabe tree.

"That one?"

"Yup." Alex turned to search the thinning line of

evergreens for her nephew Matt. Since coming home, she and Shelby had had a long talk in Shelby's kitchen and made up after their fight about Luke. Having her best friend married to her brother would require more getting used to than she'd thought, but they'd work it out fine. "It's the right size."

"It's half-*dead*."

A wry smile curled her lips. "Maybe it's just waiting for the right person to come along." She lifted her hand when she spotted Matt. The boy came running. Dressed in his Boy Scout uniform, Matt and his other troop members were holding the tree sale to help fund future field trips. "How much, kiddo?"

Matt's eyebrows disappeared beneath his bangs and a stupefied expression marked his cold-reddened cheeks. "Dad said that one was gonna be recycled. It's the top somebody cut out of a tree they bought because it wouldn't fit in their house."

Not a good fit, huh? Could it *be* any more appropriate? She and that tree were destined to spend Christmas together. "Here's a donation then," she said, pressing a twenty into Matt's pocket. "I'll carry it home."

Home. That sounded so strange. But after getting up out of that bed in Mexico a couple weeks ago and booking a flight to Tennessee, she'd stopped by David's office and turned in her notice. He'd been shocked to say the least. She'd always sworn she'd never give up her dream job, but standing here beside Shelby and Matt and looking at that sad little tree she didn't have a single regret.

She'd rented her brother Nick's old apartment above the gym, rented a storefront in the building her businessman brother had just purchased and planned to open her own photography studio January 3—if she could get the work done on time. She'd sunk most of her savings into renting both places and buying equipment and props, so the much-needed painting and cleaning had to be all hands-on.

Photographing kids and pets and weddings wouldn't be as exciting as traveling the world and capturing wolves in action, but that was okay. She was ready for the next stage of her life.

The grown-up stage.

"Sure you don't want me and Luke to drop you off?"

She shook her head at Shelby's query. "Thanks anyway, but I want to walk by the studio again."

"It hasn't changed since you left it an hour ago," Shelby teased.

"I know, but I forgot to measure the window and I want to put up white lights after I get the painting done." She gave Shelby a hug. "I'll be working on it all day tomorrow but I'll see you for the ultrasound."

Alex took her time on the walk home. The sun had set a half hour ago, and the air was crisp and cold, with the tiniest of snowflakes drifting down from the sky. No accumulation was expected but it definitely made for a pretty sight amongst the colorful Christmas lights and displays gracing the mostly empty streets.

That would take some getting used to. All the shops closed at six when she was used to having twenty-four-hour availability in the touristy towns where she traveled.

Carrying her three-foot twig beneath the ornamented streetlights, Alex took the longer route down Main

Street and window-shopped as she made her way back to her apartment via the studio. Rounding the corner off Main, she came upon the building. Squeezed in between two larger ones, it had once been a mom-and-pop grocery, then an attorney's office, then a small clothing store. Quaint and cute, it was full of potential with lots of decorative trim and old-fashioned appeal.

Alex stood and pictured the exterior painted a deep red, the entry door a glossy ebony, and black-and-white portraits on display in the window and hanging from the ceiling.

She did a quick guestimate of the size, figuring four boxes of white lights would do. It was perfect, it would *be* perfect. Heck, she might even get a dog. A big cream-colored Lab that would keep her company, was good with kids and didn't mind wearing a bow or a bonnet every now and again.

Smiling at the thought, she stepped off the curb and crossed the street, her thoughts focused entirely on her new venture and getting through Christmas with her family when she kept catching them staring at her with pity in their eyes.

That was the thing with family. She didn't have to say a word but they knew how she felt. And since she had confided to Shelby about falling in love with Dylan, it didn't take a rocket scientist to figure out Shelby had given enough information to the rest of them that they'd filled in the blanks. They were giving her space for now but she knew her reprieve wouldn't last long.

Alex approached her apartment from the rear, her head down as she dodged slippery puddles and contemplated some sarcastic comebacks for her brothers when they inevitably pulled her aside and talked about kicking Dylan's ass for breaking her heart.

Almost at the stairs, Alex gasped when she saw a man step out of the shadows.

Alex jumped back, clutching the bit of pine to her chest like a droopy little shield. Then she realized who it was.

"I didn't mean to startle you," Dylan said, raising his hands as though to smooth over the fright he'd given her.

She blinked, hardly daring to believe her eyes. Barely daring to breathe in case he disappeared. He looked so different, his beard gone. "You're *here?*"

"I couldn't stay away. Colt and I are both here," he said, tilting his head toward the car parked in the alley. "We came for the woman we both love."

He loved her. They both loved her. So much Dylan had braved the crowds and airports and come all the way from Alaska without his beard?

She knew what it meant. He wasn't hiding. Not anymore. Dylan had shown the world his face, stepped out of his prison.

For her. Because he loved her.

Alex tossed the tree aside and flew toward him, launching herself at Dylan and catching a glimpse of his smile before he wrapped his arms around her and lifted her off her feet, burying his face in her hair.

He was here. They would work their problems and issues out later. But he was here.

And that was all that mattered.

CHAPTER TWENTY-ONE

DYLAN OPENED HIS EYES and from behind the veil of Alexandra's hair he saw the streetlights at the end of the alley. The light at the end of the tunnel?

He was so tired. Tired of hiding, tired from the long trip and the nerves he'd experienced wondering if someone would recognize him, what he'd say if they did.

But no one had. And now he was with Alexandra. He wanted time to stand still.

"I love you, too," she whispered, kissing his cheek, his mouth, pressing her lips to his. "I missed you so much. I can't believe you're *here*. And your beard is gone, I like it gone. You look hot," she said with a teasing grin, "and you're here," she repeated again, as though she couldn't quite believe it.

In a way he couldn't quite wrap his mind around it, either. After two years of hiding, it felt strange to be so exposed. "Don't ever walk out like that again," he ordered, his voice husky because he'd come so close to losing her forever.

There was a scuffle from within the rental car parked behind him. He would have liked more time to talk to Alexandra alone before Colt woke up from his travel-induced nap but one of the doors swung open wide.

Dylan set her on her feet and they both turned to face the car.

"Alex!"

Dylan heard Alexandra's sharp gasp. Her mouth dropped open in shocked surprise before she caught Colt to her, hugging him and kissing him, her laughter filling the air.

"You're *talking?*" Alexandra eased Colt away and palmed his face. "Oh, sweetie, say my name again. Please?"

"Alex," Colt whispered shyly. He lifted his hands and showed her the horse she'd bought for him. "Can we see Bandit?"

Another beautiful, happy laugh bubbled from her, a laugh he'd missed more than he'd ever thought possible. "Colt missed you," he said, wrapping his arm around her. "We both did."

Her expression was soft, more than a little dazed. He could tell she was surprised. But did she want them there? Was it too much to show up like this after weeks of silence?

"How did you find me?"

He couldn't help but smile at that. It was funny how life worked sometimes. "The address on the packet you sent. I didn't see the apartment at first so I stopped in the gym to ask about you and the woman assumed I was asking about having Colt's picture taken."

Alexandra flashed a smile similar to the one she'd worn when she'd caught the fish. "Did that surprise you?"

Considering how she'd talked about traveling to get away from her family, yes. He wasn't sure what he felt about her putting down firm roots in a town he'd never heard of before meeting her but considering the size, maybe it would work.

Shaking his head at himself, he sighed. It *had* to work. "May we come in?"

She hesitated a long moment, a mixture of fear and hope flickering across her face. But without a word she led the way, carting the dying bit of pine with her.

Dylan urged Colt up the stairs, following Alexandra as she unlocked the door and left the tree on the tile by the hall table where she dropped her purse.

Knowing the time had come, Dylan squatted down in front of Colt. "Okay, Colt, this is it. Remember what we talked about on the way here? About how Alexandra and I need to talk about grown-up stuff and how you *have* to stay put?" He waited until Colt nodded. "I want you to play while Alexandra and I talk, okay? You stay in this room, right here."

Alexandra looked confused by his insistence with Colt's whereabouts, but that was a subject to be explained later. And he'd be damned sure she didn't think for a second the only reason he'd come was because Colt had run away. He'd braved airports and city traffic to see her, all because *he* loved her. This wasn't only for Colt. Now he had to find the words that had been missing for so long.

"How about a movie?" Alexandra walked over to the television. "My nephew left some of his behind when he moved out."

With efficient movements Alexandra put a DVD into the machine and seconds later Colt was ensnared by Disney magic.

With one last look at his son, Dylan followed her into the kitchen. Where to begin? "I saw the review."

"I'm sorry."

"I'm not."

She blinked at him, visibly confused. "I thought you'd be angry."

"I was. I was furious—until I remembered I couldn't throw stones. Even though you knew who I was and had pictures, you didn't use them."

"I would never do that."

"I know that, too."

She closed her eyes briefly and inhaled. "We're a pair, aren't we?"

That they were. But it was nice, too, knowing he wasn't the only one with rough edges. "I realize given the arrest and suspicion that withholding my identity from you was much more serious than you not revealing your job."

"We were both wrong, Dylan. We weren't to that point in our relationship yet and I understand why you didn't tell me. I admit, I was freaked out because I did remember, but...I get it. You didn't want that label attached and you knew it would be. What I don't understand is what changed? Don't get me wrong, I'm so glad you're here. But *why* are you here?"

Dylan tugged her body against his. "Because I wanted to look you in the eyes when I say you're right, I have been hiding. Thanks to you and Colt, it's finally sunk in that I don't want to be the last man in the bubble," he said drily, trying to smile but not quite managing it. "I don't want him growing up resenting me and thinking I'm holding him back, or wondering if the rumors are true because of how I act or where I live."

Her stance relaxed a bit. "Go on."

He stared into her upturned face, memorizing every feature, thanking God she'd ignored him and got on the Beaver that day. "Alexandra, there's something else I haven't told you. I haven't told anyone, not even Zeke. But I'm here, and I want you, but you need to know what we could be up against and...why I felt the need to hide."

SEEING THE LOOK ON HIS FACE and hearing the tone that he used, Alexandra's heart began to beat too fast. "What do you mean?"

"You've probably read the articles about me on the Internet."

She'd read them all. Page after page, site after site. It had taken a *long* time.

"Sweetheart, the man Lauren was with that night—it wasn't the first time she'd cheated."

She gripped his coat, appalled by what he was saying. She couldn't imagine being with Dylan and doing such a thing. Why take vows if you had no intention of keeping them?

Alex felt his pain, his humiliation. She remembered the photograph in the back of his novel, the arrogance. That arrogance was gone now and in its place was a man matured by life.

"I told you we had problems but Lauren and I stayed together. She got pregnant with Colt, and...everything seemed okay. Then I found out she was cheating on me. And even though she retracted her words later and claimed she'd only said them in anger, she'd once screamed that Colt wasn't mine."

Dylan loved Colt as only a father could. Not his?

How could he not know for sure? "You haven't taken a test?" Wouldn't that be the first step?

"No. I couldn't risk it. There is always a paper trail, no matter how confidential."

"You're afraid someone will find out and bring up his paternity."

"And take him away," he added, holding her gaze and nodding slowly. "Regardless of what happened between me and Lauren, I've always thought of Colt as my son and I always will. I don't care if he's not my flesh and blood, he's the only good thing to come from that disaster of a marriage.

"If the truth is known, how is he going to feel if his mother's lovers start coming out of the woodwork?" He swore softly. "After the fire, Colt was all I could think about. He'd lost his mother, his home. I hadn't loved Lauren the way a man should love his wife. But I loved Colt. I learned what was important. And right or wrong, I know if someone finds out, there are idiots out there who would come forward for their fifteen minutes of fame or a payoff."

Dylan was right. There was a huge chance of that happening. Sex tapes, DNA tests. Scandal seemed to make the world go round.

"After everything Colt had been through, I couldn't put him through that. And I couldn't risk losing him. When I sat in that jail cell and everyone was going nuts plotting out how I'd allegedly murdered her, I decided that no matter what Lauren had done, Colt was mine. I was going to be the father he needed. But as you so accurately pointed out, I haven't done a good job of that."

"You've done a wonderful job. Despite all he's been

through, Colt is a sweet, caring little boy." She couldn't imagine a better father than Dylan.

"Alexandra, sweetheart, I love you. I want to be with you. I have no more secrets." He trailed his knuckles down her cheek. "But I'm begging you to keep this one. Don't ever repeat what I've told you, for all our sakes."

The words made her heart sing even as sadness cut deep. Dylan was trying to protect Colt, yes, but Dylan was so very afraid that he didn't see that not knowing was worse than the actual truth.

She stood on tiptoe and pulled his head low, nuzzling against him, pressing a soft kiss on his lips meant to comfort and support. "I love you." She whispered the words against his mouth. "I love you," she repeated, lifting her lashes to meet and hold his gaze. "Your secrets are my secrets. But, Dylan, you've come all this way, and it'll all be for nothing if you can't face Colt's paternity, too."

Dylan closed his eyes, pain etched on his face. "What if he's not mine?"

Such a raw, bare whisper. "He's *ours* no matter what the test says. No matter what it says, we'll face it together because neither one of us is alone anymore. We have each other. We *love* each other. Don't you want to know? Don't you want to be prepared and build your defenses if the day comes that it's questioned?"

Silence.

Alex watched as Dylan looked away, withdrawing from her even as his hands pulled her closer to him. She waited, she *prayed*. But Dylan didn't speak.

Alex fingered the hair at his collar. "As a writer it's all too easy to think of all the scenarios, but what about Colt's feelings in this? What about having that knowl-

edge ahead of time if a medical issue comes up? God
forbid it happen, but if that day came and Colt found out
you've known all this time… Even though you're *the
best* father he could ever have, he would feel betrayed."

"I don't want anyone to know. It's too risky."

For a lot of reasons he'd just stated, that was true.
But… "I can help you."

"How?"

She raked her nails lightly over the softness of his face,
amazed at the heat that unfurled within her from the feel
of his skin. "My father's a doctor. He could perform a
DNA test for you. He can take the samples so we'd know
it's accurate. No one would ever know but us."

"And him. That's not the way to impress the father
of the woman I want to marry."

She was debating kissing him again and how out of
hand it could get with Colt so near when Dylan said the
words, but she froze as they sank in. "Marry?"

"You said you love me. Will you have me? Marry me?"

Marriage? She could only imagine her family's
response to the suddenness of it. "We've almost spent
more time apart than we had together."

"It's not quantity but quality that counts."

She gave him a quick, sweet kiss for that. "I agree."
Because they'd lived a lifetime in those three weeks.
Sometimes you just knew. "I will marry you. But I don't
want to rush."

Her words brought out one of Dylan's smiles, all the
more glorious because there was nothing to distract
from it now. "Whatever you want, so long as you agree."

"What about you? Will you agree to talk to my dad
about the test?"

Dylan remained silent for so long she knew he was going to refuse. She should let him handle this in his own way but he was so close to freedom and she wanted to help him take that final step. Still, he had reasons for concern and she wouldn't blame him for balking. Everything in its time.

A deep sigh left his chest and Dylan lowered his head and brushed her mouth with a kiss, delving inside when she parted for him. She would never get tired of his kisses, never get tired of that *zing* she felt every time he looked at her.

"Yes," he whispered. "I want this to be our new start. If you're by my side I can face anything."

"I hope so because it's Christmas and at some point you'll have to meet my family." She made a face. "Let me say now that I'm sorry."

"For what?"

Alexandra groaned softly. "You'll understand when you meet them," she said as she kissed him again.

SOME POINT CAME THE VERY NEXT morning when Alexandra took him and Colt to her studio. She'd already purchased paint and the needed supplies and since they couldn't spend the *entire* time in bed—Colt required food, supervision and entertainment—Dylan had volunteered his services to paint the interior.

Alexandra had taken Colt into the back with her to carry rollers and extension rods. The two of them were making quite a bit of noise rustling through bags and boxes she'd stashed out of the way. That's why he didn't hear the door open.

Giving the paint one final stir, Dylan suddenly

realized he was being watched. He turned to find several women carrying plastic containers of food, studying him with varying expressions of surprise, interest and out-and-out animosity. Into the building behind them came a troop of dark-haired men carrying ladders, buckets, toolboxes and more.

Once they were all assembled in a semicircle Dylan was being stared at by no less than twenty people. He straightened slowly. "Hello."

"Who are you?" asked one of the women.

Her gaze slipped to his hands before moving back to his face. That glance was all it took to make him realize she already knew who he was. Asking was a formality.

Alexandra's studio wasn't the O.K. Corral but this was definitely a showdown. He was outnumbered. They all loved Alexandra, so he tried to get a handle on his unease. She'd obviously told her family enough about him that they questioned his reasons for being here and his presence in Alexandra's life. But Alexandra loved him and he knew she would stand her ground. Her family might not like him or the events it had taken to get them to this place, but they'd better get damned used to having him around.

Cycling through the many descriptions of family and friends Alexandra had given him the night before, he focused on the most tension-filled face and said, "Shelby, right?"

The woman's gaze narrowed even more.

"Was it the sparks flying out of her eyes that tipped him off?" someone asked in a stage whisper.

Several of them smirked but no one laughed.

"You can't take her," said one of the younger boys. "Aunt Alex just moved back."

Dylan forced himself to meet the accusing gazes of her family. "We'll be traveling to Alaska—"

"She won't get to see me play ball!"

"Now wait a minute—"

"Are they getting married?"

"It's too soon."

"She's knocked up."

"I think it's sweet."

"Dammit, Tobias, that's our sister you're talking about!"

"Stop!" Alexandra said, her voice laced with exasperation as she walked back into the room. "Tobias, I'm *not* pregnant. And thanks for starting that rumor." She set down the items she carried on the floor, instructing Colt to do the same before she took Colt's hand and pulled him along with her to stand at Dylan's side. "What are you all doing here?"

"What's *he* doing here, Lex?" Shelby slid him another glare.

"I asked first." Alexandra waited with an impatient shift of her weight, leaning against his side.

The oldest of the group smiled. "We came to give you your homecoming present, dear. You can't possibly do all the work yourself so we came to help you."

"Oh, Gram. That is so sweet."

"Alex, you're okay? What's going on?"

Alexandra's hand slipped into his and squeezed.

"I'm fine, Dad. Better than fine now," she said with a glance up at Dylan. "Thank you all for coming. I really appreciate it. We both do."

"We?" Shelby asked pointedly.

"Yes, we. Dylan and I are together."

"You're Dylan MacGregor."

Remembering Alexandra's father was a fan, Dylan nodded and prepared himself for censure. "Bower's my last name. MacGregor is my middle name."

"We understood you've been living in Alaska for several years. Are you taking Alexandra back to Alaska with you?" her father asked.

Dylan took in the expressions on all their faces and knew he walked a thin line of acceptance. Screw it up, say the wrong thing and he'd never make it out from under the pile of male bodies taking swings at him. But say the right thing... "We will definitely be *visiting* Alaska because my father lives there but—" Dylan squeezed Alexandra's hand before releasing it and sliding his arm around her shoulders "—we're living here. And so it's clear," he said, directing his statement to her parents, "I love Alexandra and I intend to marry her as soon as she agrees to set a date."

"Sounds possessive, don't he?"

"Doesn't have a freaking clue who he's taking on."

Alexandra glared at the two guys Dylan assumed were her brothers.

"And you're okay?" Shelby asked. "Really?"

Dylan could see the worry on Shelby's face and knew his fiancée's best friend asked out of love. That made it acceptable. The size of her family would take some getting used to but he'd do it.

"I'm wonderful. Sometimes you just know when it's right."

"I think I just puked a little—*ow*, Megan, that hurt. Kiss it and make it better?"

"Will you two get a room?"

"Enough," Alexandra's father said with a shake of his head.

"Yes, boys, there are children present. Such as this little man. Alex, you need to introduce us, dear," Gram said.

Alexandra tugged Colt in front of them and glanced at Dylan again, giving him a look that stated loud and clear she had his back regardless of what the DNA test said.

"Everyone, this is Colt, my son."

EPILOGUE

One year later...

DYLAN SAT BACK IN THE OFFICE desk chair located above
Alexandra's photography studio. Now painted a bold
red, they'd bought the building from her brother Nick,
remodeled it and lived on the second and third floors
while their house was being built.

Alexandra and Colt's laughter drifted to him from
downstairs, comforting and happy as they waited for
him to finish writing for the day so they could take
Delilah out for her evening walk.

Following in her brothers' footsteps with their
penchant for marriages on holidays, he and Alexandra
had tied the knot on July Fourth at her parents' house.
Independence Day. It seemed fitting since he'd never
felt more free in his life.

Turned out he had been recognized in the airport in
Atlanta last year when he'd come to see Alexandra. Two
days after Christmas and his arrival in Beauty, articles
had appeared in the rags and news of the fire resurfaced
with photos of him snuggling a sleepy Colt close as he
walked the airport terminal. This time the stories had
taken a surprisingly positive turn and he was labeled as

being the wrongly accused father who'd nearly lost it all and—quite visibly—now cherished it.

The stories were embarrassingly incorrect on other aspects of his life but it didn't matter. His book sales had soared once again and the photos quickly disappeared when some Hollywood hottie was caught cheating on her boyfriend. His reappearance became old news.

His editor had e-mailed him after the sighting. His agent, too. He'd ignored them all and focused on one thing: his family. Never again would he lose sight of what was really important.

Ansel and Walter had moved to Alaska to help Zeke run the lodge and the three old coots were having a blast. They'd hired Sam to cover the flights and spike camps for hunters during the season, and focused their talents on fishing and the telling of tall tales.

Dylan worried about Zeke's health but knowing Ansel was there gave Dylan comfort.

Colt's childish giggle filled the air again, and Dylan smiled at the sound. How many times had he begged God to hear Colt laugh again? Now he was. Every day.

Colt was receiving counseling at Beauty's hospital and had gone from being withdrawn and leery to happy and boisterous in a matter of months.

Only one thing kept Dylan from total satisfaction.

His writing.

Writers write. It's what they did. Scenes, dialogue, characters. The different characteristics appeared at will, impatient to be put to paper and created. And since November, ever since meeting Alexandra, he'd done that, hammering out the story of Evangeline and her gunslinger cowboy and their thrilling adventure to the

Klondike following the trail of a killer. The story had it all. Mystery, suspense, romance. Aspects that would appeal to a broad audience.

This was it. This was his comeback book if he chose to put it out there. All he had to do was be brave enough to e-mail his agent and start the process. Alexandra and her family supported him. Believed in him.

And now that a very discreet, very nerve-racking paternity test proved Colt was indeed his, nothing held him back but himself.

Hands shaking, Dylan clicked to send a new e-mail, added his agent's name as the recipient and attached the file, but hesitated over the body of the letter.

What to write when he hadn't spoken to the man since the fire? When he'd ignored the calls and e-mails and letters lending support and asking for contact?

Finally it came to him.

Sorry it took so long.
I hope it was worth the wait.

* * * * *

Harlequin offers a romance for every mood!
See below for a sneak peek
from our paranormal romance line
Silhouette® Nocturne™.
Enjoy a preview of REUNION by USA TODAY
bestselling author Lindsay McKenna.

Aella closed her eyes and sensed a distinct shift, like movement from the world around her to the unseen world.

She opened her eyes. And had a slight shock at the man standing ten feet away. He wasn't just any man. Her heart leaped and pounded. He reminded her of a fierce warrior from an ancient civilization. Incan? She wasn't sure but she felt his deep power and masculinity.

I'm Aella. Are you the guardian of this sacred site? she asked, hoping her telepathy was strong.

Fox's entire body soared with joy. Fox struggled to put his personal pleasure aside.

Greetings, Aella. I'm the assistant guardian to this sacred area. You may call me Fox. How can I be of service to you, Aella? he asked.

I'm searching for a green sphere. A legend says that the Emperor Pachacuti had seven emerald spheres created for the Emerald Key necklace. He had seven of his priestesses and priests travel the world to hide these spheres from evil forces. It is said that when all seven spheres are found, restrung and worn, that Light will return to the Earth. The fourth sphere is here, at your sacred site. Are you aware of it? Aella held her breath.

She loved looking at him, especially his sensual mouth. The desire to kiss him came out of nowhere.

Fox was stunned by the request. *I know of the Emerald Key necklace because I served the emperor at the time it was created. However, I did not realize that one of the spheres is here.*

Aella felt sad. Why? Every time she looked at Fox, her heart felt as if it would tear out of her chest. *May I stay in touch with you as I work with this site?* she asked.

Of course. Fox wanted nothing more than to be here with her. To absorb her ephemeral beauty and hear her speak once more.

Aella's spirit lifted. What *was* this strange connection between them? Her curiosity was strong, but she had more pressing matters. In the next few days, Aella knew her life would change forever. How, she had no idea....

Look for REUNION
by USA TODAY bestselling author
Lindsay McKenna,
available April 2010, only from
Silhouette® Nocturne™.

HARLEQUIN® Romance®

ROMANCE, RIVALRY
AND A FAMILY REUNITED

THE BRIDES
of
BELLA ROSA

William Valentine and his beloved wife, Lucia, live
a beautiful life together, but when his former love Rosa
and the secret family they had together resurface,
an instant rivalry is formed. Can these families
get through the past and come together as one?

*Step into the world of Bella Rosa
beginning this April with*

Beauty and the Reclusive Prince
by
RAYE MORGAN

Eight volumes to collect and treasure!

www.eHarlequin.com

HR17650

OLIVIA GATES

BILLIONAIRE, M.D.

Dr. Rodrigo Valderrama has it all…
everything but the woman he's secretly
desired and despised. A woman forbidden
to him—his brother's widow.
And she's pregnant.

Cybele was injured in a plane crash
and lost her memory. All she knows is
she's falling for the doctor who has swept her
away to his estate to heal. If only the secrets
in his eyes didn't promise to tear
them forever apart.

Available March wherever you buy books.

Always Powerful, Passionate and Provocative.

Silhouette®

SPECIAL EDITION

INTRODUCING A BRAND-NEW MINISERIES FROM *USA TODAY* BESTSELLING AUTHOR

KASEY MICHAELS

SECOND-CHANCE BRIDAL

At twenty-eight, widowed single mother Elizabeth Carstairs thinks she's left love behind forever....until she meets Will Hollingsbrook. Her sons' new baseball coach is the handsomest man she's ever seen—and the more time they spend together, the more undeniable the connection between them. But can Elizabeth leave the past behind and open her heart to a second chance at love?

FIND OUT IN

SUDDENLY A BRIDE

Available in April
wherever books are sold.

HARLEQUIN
Super Romance

COMING NEXT MONTH

Available April 13, 2010